O MY DARLING

O MY DARLING

A NOVEL

BY

Amity Gaige

Other Press • New York

Two excerpts from this novel were first published in altered forms by *Epoch*—1999 (Vol. 48, No. 3) and 2001 (Vol. 50, No. 1)—for which permission is gratefully acknowledged.

Production Editor: Robert D. Hack
Text design: Natalya Balvova
This book was set in Janson Text by Alpha Graphics of Pittsfield, NH.

10 9 8 7 6 5 4 3 2 1

Library of Congress Cataloging-in-Publication Data

Gaige, Amity, 1972-
    O my darling / by Amity Gaige.
        p. cm.
    ISBN 1-59051-174-3 (hardcover : alk. paper) 1. Home ownership–Fiction.
2. Married people–Fiction. 3. Young adults–Fiction. I. Title.
    PS3557 .A3518O17 2005
    813'.54–dc22
                                                    2004019260

for Tim

Earth's the right place for love;
I don't know where it's likely to go better.

—Robert Frost

PART ONE

BIRTHDAY

"Tell me," she said.

"No," he said.

"Come on," she was laughing. "Just tell me what it is."

"No," he said. "You have to guess."

"Guess? Guess?" She had both hands on her head. "I hate guessing. You know that. Just give it to me."

"I want you to guess," Clark said evenly, holding the gift behind his back. The young couple, Clark and Charlotte Adair, stood in the middle of their kitchen, which they had yesterday painted yellow. Everything was still in boxes all around the house, for they had just moved in.

Although he spoke casually enough, Clark was weak with excitement—today was a birthday. Today was a day to honor childhood, which he remembered as something like a galaxy of sweets and coincidences. This was a day to feel as precious and doted upon as one tended to feel as a child, as precious and doted upon as *he* had felt at least, and to forget altogether that one was grown up. Birthdays. He remembered the body heat of his parents behind him as he beckoned the party guests in from the rain. Though Clark was not yet thirty, he would be soon, and what struck him about adulthood so far was the sheer quantity of issues that arose of their own accord, no matter how pleasantly you behaved. Too many issues to name. Today was a birthday. A day to put all that aside.

"OK," Charlotte said, shrugging. She took two steps backward and looked at her husband, finger in mouth. Suddenly she seemed happy to comply.

"Flowers," she said.

"Nope," said Clark, aware of an immediate look of relief on her face. "Flowers are for normal days. Today is your birthday."

"Well, what did you *get* me?" She was blushing. The sight of her pale face with blooming cheeks transfixed him. They were both very tall and lean, like two halves of the same thing. But where Charlotte was fair, Clark's coloring bore the trace of shadows, with his dark curls and a faintly Arabian nose. Charlotte drew her sucked-pink finger from her mouth.

"Why are you smiling?" she said.

"God damn," he said, almost involuntarily. "You look beautiful. Beautiful like a child. It's amazing. You look like you're about seven. And you've just come in from playing outside."

"I'd never want to be seven again," said Charlotte.

"No no," Clark said, quickly. "Seven in *spirit*."

"I'd never want to be seven again," said Charlotte, "especially in spirit."

"Well, what I meant was," Clark shifted the present behind his back, "you look happy. I like to see you happy."

Charlotte lowered her gaze to Clark's navel. Her face grew

serious. With one finger, she drew a tendril of lank blonde hair out of her eyes. She appeared to be trying to see the birthday present through his body.

She looked up. "I hope you didn't get me something too extravagant," she said. "I said no extravagance this year. With the new house . . ."

Clark's extravagance with money was sometimes an issue, but for him to bring up her bringing it up would have been a whole new, collateral issue. Today was a birthday. (Charlotte's birthday, though did it matter whose in a marriage?) A day to remember the hunger one felt as a child for each new thing, each singular word, and each honest daybreak. He fondled the gift box behind his back.

"It's not extravagant," he said.

"OK," she said, looking up at the ceiling. "It's not flowers, and it's not extravagant."

What is it, Charlotte Adair thought, out of all things? A gift. A birthday gift. Suddenly, she found herself believing that inside this small box was one of the fantastical gifts on some long ago wish list—a harp, a pony, a castle. The thought made her giddy. She felt that she was at the center of everything. She was the birthday girl. The gift was for her. She closed her eyes and felt the rupturing pressure of laughter in her chest. But just then, her eyes snapped open. She was afraid to stand there with her eyes closed, like a child praying to God. She looked around suspiciously at the strange new kitchen. Then she looked at her husband's shadowed face—almond colored, pretty-eyed. What if for some reason he was pulling her leg?

"Let me see it," she said.

"No way," laughed Clark. "You'll guess right away if you see it."

She stepped back. She took a deep breath. Of course he wasn't pulling her leg. He liked giving presents. He liked birthdays.

"Is it . . . ," she said, "another figurine?"

Clark fondled the gift again. It was not a figurine, because the figurine had definitely been an issue last year. He agreed now that the figurine had been a strange gift, something suited better for a child. But it had looked so much *like* her, he still wanted to protest, a porcelain maiden wringing out her long, long hair.

"Nope," he said. "It's absolutely not a figurine."

"Hey," Charlotte said, looking up at him flirtatiously. "Did you get me that necklace I saw at Shand's the other day? Did you sneak back over there and buy that necklace for me?"

It took Clark a moment to remember the necklace they had seen together.

"No," he said. "Listen, I didn't get you jewelry."

"OK," said Charlotte. "Then can I have it now?"

"Come on," said Clark. "Use your imagination."

But as soon as he said the word "imagination" he knew he had chosen the wrong word. Since they'd begun moving in, Charlotte's lack of imagination had become an issue. She would stare at the empty rooms, blinking, unable to envision. Clark felt that she was unable to let go of the expected places and uses for things. She was unable to dream, unable to guess. The week previous, he had gone so far as to call her "boring," and to prove that she was not boring, she took everything back out of the kitchen cabinets and dashed them against the wall. Among other things, such as all of his mother's china, she had broken the birthday figurine, and in that case, thought Clark, the figurine wasn't such a hot thing for her to bring up either.

Charlotte's eyes darkened. She too remembered the incident with the china. She saw the white plates flying like epithets toward the wall. Although they'd had their tussles, they had never fought like that, never thrown anything, and now their first house was anointed in a shower of porcelain. She felt very bad about it and also implicitly reaccused. She took a deep breath. She tried to remember that today was her birthday, a day to claim one's place at the center of everything before one has to step aside for the next of six billion people, a day to feel cosmically attractive, a day to feel wanted, and she tried to get back to that dreamy, closed-eyed feeling of the birthday girl.

But instead she said, helpless to stop herself, "Is it a rope to hang myself with?"

Suddenly, the issues abounded: Charlotte's rather dark sense of humor, her inability to behave sportingly, and more disastrously, the horribly recent death of Clark's mother, which had been a suicide.

Charlotte's eyes flew open when she realized what she had said.

"Just kidding," she said. "Oh God. It was a joke. I wasn't thinking. It was an innocent joke."

Clark still held the birthday gift behind his back. His eyes flickered momentarily, but his expression did not change.

"Are you going to guess for real or not?" he asked.

Charlotte looked down. Softly she said, "I guessed for real already, Clark."

"Just twice? That's all the guesses you've got in you?"

"Can't I just *have* it?" said Charlotte.

"But this is the best part," he said, "the guessing. Listen," the gift box—covered sloppily in striped wrapping paper—hung now at his side. "You don't enjoy your birthday, Charlotte. You always get sad on your birthday. I thought I'd try to make it fun this year."

They both stood silently for a moment. It was true, about Charlotte and birthdays. She was trying very hard to be the birthday girl but she couldn't stick with it. Outside, the dog gave one of his long, heartbroken howls. They could hear him dragging his chain back and forth across the patio. Clark looked at the floor and Charlotte looked out the window. Outside, the hawthorn tree shook its angry naked branches.

"February," Charlotte sighed. "Why did I have to be born in the sorriest month of the year?"

"See?" said Clark, "There you go, getting sad."

"A lot of times, with adopted children, they just make up the birthday. I mean, sometimes they don't know. So maybe I wasn't even born today. I've never seen my birth certificate. They might have just fudged the papers at the agency. Maybe I was filling their February quota."

"That's it," Clark gestured with his shoulder. "The gift is related to the time of year. Understand? You're getting warm."

"A raincoat?" Charlotte squinted.

"No," said Clark, putting the box behind his back again. It was then he realized that a raincoat was what he should have gotten. A raincoat would have been a lot better than the stupid thing he had gotten. His arms hurt, holding the gift on and on this way. And yet it seemed too late to just give it to her.

"Ohhh," she said. "I know."

A smile arose on Charlotte's face, and for a moment, Clark felt very badly. She guessed that the gift was two tickets to go see the ballet *Giselle* that was being performed in a nearby city, something she had hinted at wanting several times but which was wrong. Then, undeterred, she guessed a scarf, then an umbrella, both of which were wrong but were, in fact, related to the time of year. She guessed a number of reasonable things, and Clark noticed that each one would have made a better gift than the stupid gift he'd gotten and that all of them were wrong. He had thought long and hard about what present to buy his wife this year, and yet none of those reasonable things had come to mind. He listened, looking at the kitchen walls, which still smelled fresh and wet with paint, his arms aching.

A rabbit bounced out of the hedge into the backyard. Charlotte looked at it.

"Did you get me a rabbit?" she said.

Then she began to guess whatever came to mind and at that point Clark did not stop her: a meat grinder, an egg beater, an anteater, a cheeseburger, a sheepherder, a rectal thermometer, a flower for Algernon, a purple heart, a dark horse, a bird in the hand, a burning bush, a kind word, a million-dollar idea, a guardian angel, immortal life.

"Oh Christ," she said, and began to cry.

Clark went to the pantry and put the gift box on the topmost shelf. They had forgotten to paint the pantry. He looked at the decrepit wallpaper.

"I'll give it to you later," he said aloud in the pantry.

Charlotte sat down at the breakfast table and Clark sat

down beside her. He passed her a tissue. They were silent for some time.

"We've been fighting since the day we moved into this house," said Charlotte. "We never used to fight."

"Well, let's not fight anymore then," said Clark. "It's the stress."

"There's been a lot of stress. The funeral. Going through old things. Moving in, all at the same time."

"Packing, unpacking. Painting."

"Breaking plates. So much to do." Charlotte smiled shyly, then she started to cry again.

"Don't cry," Clark said tenderly, grasping her hand.

"Why not?" she said.

"I don't know," he said. "I guess you can go ahead and have a cry."

"A birthday cry," said Charlotte, smiling a little.

"Sure," said Clark. "A birthday cry. You save up enough of those things and someday you'll have yourself a birthday river."

"My own river," said Charlotte.

Clark played with the napkin holder they had just unpacked. He lifted the small bar up and down. He pretended to guillotine the screaming napkins until he finally got her to laugh.

"Well, Charlie," said Clark. "Let me tell you. You certainly used your imagination."

Charlotte laughed again, drying her tears with a napkin. Then they looked out the window together, where the damp winds of February blew like an army of witches over the small yard.

YOU

She was gone now. But way back, when Clark was a boy, his mother had explained the world. She explained how things functioned, the secrets of things. For example, the passage of time (according to Vera Adair) was overseen by a dwarf who lived in a shack in the desert somewhere outside of Las Vegas. At night, he would hoist the moon up by a rope and pulley. In the morning, of course, he would raise the sun. And the weather? The weather was operated by a series of magical animals that lived in the mountains.

These were stories for children but she did not stop telling them. Even after Clark grew up and realized that his mother had invented everything, that little of what she said was true, even after they told him she was unwell, even after she ended her own life to drive the point home, Clark still thought of the weather in exactly the same way. When it snowed, he thought of the black bear of winter standing on a cliff, tossing the snow out of his satchel. At least once, at the start of every spring, he pictured the little lamb of spring gamboling down from the mountains to deliver the rosebuds.

It was not that Clark still believed these stories were true, he merely appreciated their familiarity. He knew he was the son of a madwoman. The years before her death were the worst. Like his father and sister, he did not cry at her funeral. And now all of them were behaving as if her death were far more than three months distant. But in secret, in some sort of inviolable compact, Clark held onto her crazy and wonderful stories, much in the same way that aging ladies held onto their handsome dead fiancés of distant wars. Even now, as the morning was breaking pinkly over his first March in his first house, paying out the light, there was this sense of magic, of tremendous unpredictability, at which his mother's stories had once hinted. He missed her. Of course he did. Also, he was relieved.

The wind fell still over the house, and the winter-naked trees rattled outside the bedroom window. I'll have to take a look at that window, Clark thought to himself. The thought made him proud: He would have to take a look at the window. Who else but him, the man of the house? Clark inhaled and smiled. He raised himself on the pillow, and looked down into his wife's face.

"Have you ever been in love?" he asked her.

Charlotte grinned sleepily. She drew her forearm across her brow. Her long hair, which was the color of sugar corn and without the slightest curl, crisscrossed the pillow. She had a small mouth and a sudden, snaggle-toothed smile. He could see the tiny ridges at the bottoms of her teeth.

"I mean," said Clark, "besides with me."

"Who says I'm in love with you?" said Charlotte.

"I don't know. Are you?"

"I'm not that kind of girl."

Clark tickled her just under the arm, and she squirmed. "Really?"

"I'm asleep," she said. "I'm *asleep*. Shall I hang a sign from my nose?"

"What about that guy who went into the military? The one who proposed to you at a Drive-Thru. Private Downyourpants."

"Who, him?" said Charlotte, rolling her eyes. "No, we weren't in love. We just happened to be running from love in the same direction."

Clark smiled. Because it was his first spring-like morning in their new house, and because his pretty young wife had teased him and was warm beside him on the bed, and because he was surviving all that had happened, it felt like the first smile of his life. Everything was wide open. Everything was first. Spring was the most hopeful season, and soon the grounds around the new house would bloom, who knew what buried flowers there were, and maybe Charlotte could finally have a garden. He was proud to own this house. He felt sure that a garden would arise immaculately out of the ground around it. He felt hopeful and young like that.

Marriage, he thought, touching his wife's hair. Marriage, what is it? Why does a person do it? Why does a person grab a girl by the shoulder as she is walking, one summer evening, turn her around and ask her to marry him? Maybe it's simply the most outrageous thing a man can do. A man can jump from buildings, a man can wrestle bulls, but inwardly he will know none of it can compare to swinging a girl round and asking her to marry him. It was irrepressible. It was outrageous. Marriage is the only punishment great enough to fit the crime of love. Clark laughed to himself, fingering Charlotte's hair. Marriage is the only punishment great enough to fit the crime of love, he thought. But of course, marriage didn't even feel like a punishment. Three years into it, it no longer even felt outrageous. Only on certain mornings, waking up next to her, did he realize what an adventure it was. A billion times it had happened before them, and yet here they were, the first.

Charlotte rolled over and put her cheek on her arm and looked at him. A faintly sweet, confectionery scent arose from her body. Knots of crusted sleep hung in her lashes. Her dark eyes were soft and engorged with dreams. She looked terribly pretty to him.

"You?" she asked him. "I bet you've been in love a million times. Give me a number, if you had to count them."

"Not a million," Clark said. "Three or four."

"Three or four million times?"

"No," said Clark, laughing and leaning back against the headboard. "Three or four times. I have fallen in love with groups of women, but I just count them once."

"Groups? Ethnic groups?"

"No, no. I fell in love with my sister's friends when I was a boy. They used to practice kissing on me. Sometimes more than kissing. I've told you about them. Janine Hoffstead. Kiki Zuckerman. Oh, Kiki," Clark sighed. "I was in love then."

"You were not in love," said Charlotte, clucking her tongue. "You knew nothing about love. You were a boy."

"Then I'm still a boy. Because I still know nothing about love. And I'm still in love."

Charlotte turned her head away, but he could tell she was smiling.

"Who is she?" she asked.

She rolled on her back and yawned, curling up her fists with the thumbs tucked in. She arched her back, her skin visible through her thin pink rayon nightgown. She stretched one consummately white leg, then she stretched the other. Her skin was so white, almost transparent at the wrists and knees. In the summer, she would carry herself about in the shade like a vial of mercury, wearing a frayed straw hat.

"You," he said.

The bear of winter grunted in his sleep. The dwarf in the desert dropped a grain of sand. The lamb of spring leapt across the clean blue sky. The sky outside was clear and new and first.

"Well," Charlotte said. "I was thinking of making jelly toast. Your father sent us some blackberry jam."

Clark paused. He looked at the walls for a moment, his eyes casting beyond them.

Finally he said, "I won't eat that. Probably his girlfriend made it, the hag."

"You're talking about Mrs. Flanigan," said Charlotte.

"Yes, Mrs. Flanigan," he answered darkly. "The home-wrecker."

"Clark," Charlotte said. "Let's not go into it."

"You asked if I wanted her blackberry jam."

"Yes, but let's not go into it. That home was wrecked long before Mrs. Flanigan came into the picture. You know that."

Clark stared at the ceiling. He wasn't listening anymore. He didn't know that.

"If you want to talk about love," he said. "If you want to talk about two people in love, talk about Mother and Dad. Way back when. Before Mrs. Flanigan. Before me. When they lived together in a chicken coop on the Rio Grande, right after they were married. When they were our age."

Charlotte sat up and reached for her robe.

"I feel a disagreement coming on," she murmured. "I think I'm coming down with a disagreement." She smiled over her shoulder, but Clark was still staring at the ceiling.

Charlotte had heard about the chicken coop half a dozen times by now. Each time it caused her pain. Not only did it pain her that he told the same story over and over with no nod to the fact that she'd already heard it, it pained her to know it was not true. Well, it was a Vera story. It contained *elements* of the truth— one malarial summer spent in Texas with a church group. The truth one had to get from Clark's father in the kitchen over a glass of bourbon. From there, on many a visit, Charlotte had watched her handsome new husband sitting on a tiny footstool in the living room, laughing and hugging his knees, while a woman in a white nightgown spoke in her protracted, actorly way, making large facial motions as if playing to a large room, and Charlotte would think yes, he loves her, but surely he doesn't *believe* her.

"I mean it was unheard of," Clark was saying, "two gringos out there on *La Frontera*. They even had a pet macaw. They called it . . ."

"Julito," whispered Charlotte, looking at her feet.

"Julito. My father helped the locals build a church at night, by the light of a thousand candles. Afterwards, they'd fall asleep watching the stars through the chicken wire . . ."

"Clark," said Charlotte. "Do you want some jelly toast? I'll make it for you. I won't use Mrs. Flanigan's jam."

But looking over at him on the bed, she saw that he was far away in his false memories, a place in which he'd been taking refuge more and more often. How *abstract* he'd become lately, she thought, how hard to reach, when what she loved about him before was his nearness, his ready-to-go-ness, how he would pull a peach out of his pocket, sit down right then and there, and they would make a picnic out of it. He was the most spontaneous person she'd ever met, always alert to some small joy, always jumping up. She had been terribly drawn to this quality, for she herself was reticent, skeptical, often overcome with a great passivity when faced with something lovely she wanted. Now, beside her, he laughed softly to himself. His head was submerged in the pillow like a dark pearl, the black curls flattened against both temples. His large, gray eyes, almost astral in their gray blueness, looked so rapt that she almost turned to see what he was looking at. But of course he was looking at nothing. He was remembering. Remembering things that had never happened.

Charlotte felt her pulse quicken. She felt stranded in the present. She didn't want to be left alone in the present in this new house. Suddenly, the house felt hollow and large and impossible to furnish. She put the robe over her shoulders and looked outside into the small backyard.

"I should work on that garden today," she said. "I should plant things."

"Mom and Dad didn't speak the language," said Clark. "But they learned how to do things sort of anthropologically. Mother learned to make milk from scratch. She learned to make milk the way the Mexicans did."

"Don't Mexicans get milk from *cows*," Charlotte said to the window, "the way everybody else does?"

Clark held up one finger instructively. "She watched, you see. She *listened*. She had the patience of a monk. And in that little schoolhouse by the creek, she would teach the local children to recite William Blake. 'It was many and many a year ago in a kingdom by the sea' . . ."

"But you weren't there, Clark," said Charlotte. "You don't know what happened between them. You can't tell what somebody else's marriage is really like. That's not even *Blake*, by the way."

And then, out of nowhere, Clark actually proceeded to recite the poem anyway, his long-fingered hands folded over his chest, "'. . . That a maiden there lived who you may know,' and so on and so on and so on."

Charlotte gripped the sheets.

"Jesus, Clark," she said. "If it was all so wonderful, then where was your *dad* when your mother died?"

Clark winced. His eyes refocused. He was back. He stared coldly at the ceiling.

"Yes, why don't you go make jelly toast?" he said. "Use Mrs. Flanigan's jam."

Charlotte lay back down on the bed and hung her head.

"Damn," she said.

She was sorry she had said that, about his mother. She felt better, but she was still sorry she had said it. She watched Clark's chest rise and fall.

"You know I'm just jealous," she said, rolling onto his chest and tickling his nipple. "I'm an orphan. I don't have all sorts of pretty childhood stories like you do. Family legends. Starlight. Candlelight."

Clark said nothing. He continued to stare at the ceiling.

"I'm really sorry," she said. "We promised we wouldn't fight."

When he still didn't answer, she murmured, "Please, Clark. I swear I'll never speak of her that way again. I'll never mention it again."

He blinked slowly and his face seemed to relax. He had long, dark eyelashes that sprouted delicately like the tines of a fish fork.

"You know, maybe you were right," Charlotte said. "Maybe they *were* in love."

"And maybe you were right," he said, turning away. "Maybe I was just a boy."

TECUMSEH

Clark's mother had left no suicide note. It might have been the one time in her life in which she had not said enough. She did leave, however, a trunkful of uncompleted crossword puzzles, a viola, a hairbrush, two hundred and two watercolor studies of the same barn, three closets of pretty silk dresses with singed holes from her Turkish cigarettes, a dozen white nightgowns, a broken seismograph, the lingering scent of valerian root, the lingering sound of her raving in anger, a piece of cake with a fork in it that had been the last thing she tasted, several heavy glass ashtrays, her china, and a dog.

Tecumseh was a shrewd, somewhat gloomy husky with a black muzzle and soft gray withers. His heavy coat was uneven, and he had the canniest way of walking sideways, like a crab. His eyes were the color of ice caps—almost white, almost the color of nothing. For as long as anyone could remember, this dog had followed his white-nightgowned mistress from room to room, a weary butler. Clark's father hated him. And perhaps the feeling was mutual. The dog, of course, had been the first to come upon the body. The dog had been found waiting with the body. In the days following the suicide, the old man and the old dog had inhabited the same ruined house, avoiding one another in the hallways. During the funeral reception, the dog howled so woefully from the backyard that it was difficult to concentrate on mourning, and the guests appeared suspicious of themselves, unsure that they felt badly enough.

Charlotte remembered the funeral in all its variety of painfulness. She remembered the dog—unkempt, apoplectic—in the backyard. She disliked dogs, but for some reason elected herself as the one to go outside and calm the animal, whose howling was upsetting everyone. She had approached across the yard with her arms out, slowly, cop-like, but as soon as she was close enough, the dog leapt up and snapped at her, its chain taut as wire.

Retreating to the patio, alone in her thin dress in the cold, Charlotte could not help but reflect on the dog's beastly loyalty. For the dead woman had never liked Charlotte, had never once been warm. Why not just admit it now that she was gone? And now Vera was dead, and it was a terrible thing, but alone in the cold on the patio of the dead woman's house, Charlotte remembered all the woman's queer, maddening, extravagant late-night requests, so many attempts to lure Clark back to her, when Charlotte had only wanted to be liked. And surely the woman knew she would lose him to *someone*, he whom she had lost now forever by her own hand! Charlotte had stood shivering in the cold, watching little white puffs come out from the dog's mouth, confused as to how she was needed. It was horrible, all of it. Suicide. Her poor tall husband, stooping now to accept kisses in quiet rooms. She would not have wished any of it on anyone. And yet she was relieved. To her own shame. Her mother-in-law's death was like the fall of a bizarre and powerful civilization of which she'd never been a part. But what did you do with the shame? Where did you put it—in what basement?

The next day, they had driven away from the house together in the sunshine. Two and a half years into their marriage, and only then did it seem to Charlotte that they were beginning, setting off truly for the first time, like honeymooners, just the two of them. Beside her, Clark seemed calm and mature in his funeral suit. He stared manfully ahead at the road. She'd put a hand on his thigh. She wanted to say I love you, but to her the phrase so often seemed to require some sort of introduction or ceremony; one did not say I love you in cars, or in buses, or when speaking of something else. Or while waiting in line. Or when one was sleepy or flatulent or bad-smelling. She blinked in the January sunlight. What did it mean that, as a grown woman, the phrase was still exotic to her?

I . . . I . . .

She turned to look back at her mother-in-law's house, so that she might see it disappear behind them forever, the house of heartache and insanity, to give it one last big *sayonara*, when instead, she was confronted with the whiskered mug of Tecumseh. She screamed.

"Clark!" Charlotte cried. "Your mother's dog is in the back of our car!"

Clark turned around and looked at the dog. "I know," he said. "Good boy."

"But I'm *allergic* to dogs!"

"No you're not," said Clark.

"I mean, I don't *like* them."

Clark smiled into the rear view mirror, as if he didn't want the dog to have to hear what was being said about him. "We're going to have to keep him," he said.

"What?" Charlotte looked back at the creature. "Why can't we take him to the pound and find some nice loving home? We barely have room in our *apart*ment."

"We're buying a house," said Clark, slipping the check out of his breast pocket, which he had just gotten from the lawyer the day before. It was stark white in the sunlight. "We're buying that house from the paper with this money that my mother left me."

Charlotte had fallen silent. She wanted a house very much, but she was shocked. As long as she'd known Clark, he'd never made such a run of firm and serious decisions. She looked over at his profile. The top of his black curly hair was sticking to the car's felt interior.

"Listen," Clark said, after a while. "I hardly took anything of hers. I didn't take her watercolors or her capes or anything. I let Mary take care of everything. They put the rest in the yard. *In the yard.*" He looked over at Charlotte, and that was when she saw a particular pallor in his eyes she had never seen before. From the backseat, Tecumseh yawned loudly. "So, I'm going to take care of the one thing left, the thing that mattered most to her. I think she would have wanted me to."

"But how could you know?" Charlotte said. "How could you know what she wanted? It was impossible to know with her. She was . . ."

Charlotte looked back at the dog. It withdrew its long pink

tongue, and appeared to stop breathing for a moment. It cocked its head, as if to say, like some street tough, You lookin' at *me*?

"I knew," said Clark. "I knew."

Charlotte looked out the window. She thought of the lonely, reverent way in which Clark had moved about his parents' house those past several days, preparing for the funeral, behaving almost as if his mother was merely napping upstairs. He did not act the way his sister and father acted. He did not act as if anything were over.

SOLD

The house they picked was yellow and squat, with a friendly, two-windowed stare. Across the street sat a tawny apple orchard full of blackbirds that yawed all day. Clark and Charlotte had seen a picture of the house in the newspaper: 12 Quail Hollow Road. They had never really owned anything together before.

When they first went to see the house, they were pleased to see that it looked just like its picture in the paper. Charlotte fell in love with the sunny kitchen and the small backyard, while Clark liked the chimney pot that muttered when the wind blew. The floors inside were herringbone parquet, and the treads on the staircase were short, like the treads of an old cabin, even though the house was not old. The backyard was bordered by evergreen hedges, and in the middle of the yard there was a single hawthorn tree that looked perpetually seized with fright.

In the upstairs bedroom, there was a fist-sized hole in the wall, the only thing the previous owners had left behind them. A hole in the wall and a number of golden hairpins stuck in the cracks between floorboards, as well as a certain perfumey after-scent that betrayed how recently the house had been vacated.

Otherwise, it was a cozy house, and appeared to be in excellent condition.

"Go ahead," said the realtor. "Throw out a number. Seize the day."

He smiled, a hairpin between his teeth.

And soon the house was theirs.

Down the hill from the house lay a small city called Clementine. This was to be their new town—a small, nondescript city watched over by an enormous glowing clock atop the city hall. Venturing through this town with its liquor stores and darkened churches and old prewar doorways with inscrutable Latin phrases carved on the lintels, they often got lost or turned around and had to ask for directions, at which point a stranger would simply gesture up toward their hill, where their new house, the place in which they suddenly belonged, lay waiting.

Several weeks after burying his mother, Clark became the new guidance counselor at Clementine Junior High School. They took a picture of him and put it up in the hallway. His expression was that of being about to speak. His head was at the very top of the frame, betraying, even in the photograph, his extraordinary tallness.

ELSEWHERE

Clark got his gypsy darkness from his mother, as well as her gray-blue eyes, but he got his height from his father. Both men were tall enough to wear Tall Man clothes. Inside houses, Clark retained the stooped, wincing look of very tall men. But outside, under the skies, he looked comfortable, loose and athletic, the white palms of his hands flapping beside him. Sometimes Clark fantasized about having a life custom built to scale—not just Tall Man ceilings and Tall Man chairs, but Tall Man luck, long as his shadow, and Tall Man grace, like Lynn Swann leaping out over the end zone as if it were a clearing of heather, and a Tall Man's ability to know what to say.

For example, one night in bed with Charlotte that first spring, soon after moving into the house on Quail Hollow Road, he was seized with a strange feeling he could not explain. It was a feeling of being elsewhere. He did not feel he was actually in the bed, in the house, making love with his wife, but rather looking back at his young body with an old man's eyes. Sorrow washed over him. He pulled away from Charlotte's embrace and sat upright naked at the edge of the bed.

Clark was already prone to nostalgia. He missed many things merely because they were over. And because he missed them, he assumed they had been good things. He missed his boyhood. He missed the town of Carnifex Ferry where he had been raised until six years of age, before a succession of misunderstandings regarding his mother had sent them to other towns. That night, visions of Carnifex Ferry flooded him—a baseball sailing out over a fence, an idling bookmobile, Sno-Cones being lowered into hands, people running inside from the rain. He realized that he could remember that town in precise detail even though he could not remember anything but a shadow of the past year, and he missed it and he missed the summers his family spent at the nearby lake, where, on his fifteenth birthday, he lost his virginity to Kiki Zuckerman in a lean-to. That same day, he'd burst his eardrum while diving off a drawbridge, which lent the love act a dreamy impossibility that he never quite forgot. Suddenly, he missed being a virgin. He was nostalgic for the enormity of small moments. This nostalgia was so oppressive that he felt as if he'd become an old man in the space of an hour.

He looked over at his mother's dog, who had moved demurely to the corner of the bedroom during the lovemaking but was now staring back at him through the darkness with his reflective eyes. When Clark turned forward again, he saw—he swore it—a lithe feminine shadow pass casually across the bedroom doorway.

"What—" he said, and then stopped. He looked back at Charlotte, who still lay prone on the bed, awake but motionless. He slapped his hand to his head. Clearly, there was nothing there.

Shadows. Still, he turned his head toward the dark opacity that filled the door, staring hard at it for several long moments.

Charlotte cleared her throat.

"Get me some brandy, would you be a doll," she said.

Clark looked over his shoulder. Behind him, she lay on the bed with her knees closed conclusively. They had been silent for some time.

"I really don't feel like being a doll right now," he said.

"Fine," she said, "don't be a doll and get me some brandy anyway."

He lay down, reached insincerely for her in the dark, and then covered his feet, which were cold and hanging off the edge of the bed. He wanted to say he was sorry. He didn't say anything. *Never apologize*, came his father's voice from a hundred occasions of his youth. The old man had passed on to Clark, like an heirloom, a pointed, almost righteous resistance to the act of apologizing. *Do what you did or don't have done it.* In the silence, Clark looked down at his interminable legs. Charlotte was very quiet but he could tell she was still awake.

"Do you think there are ghosts in this house?" he said.

"Oh God," Charlotte said, "If you're going to talk about ghosts, I really need some brandy."

"Don't worry," said Clark. "I'm kidding. I don't believe in ghosts."

But, just to be sure, he looked out at the empty doorway. Then he touched the back of Charlotte's night-darkened hair. Her shoulder was cupped by moonlight.

"Hey," he said.

After a while, he kicked back the sheets and went to get the brandy, ducking under the doorjamb. He came out into the hall and looked around. Without turning on the lights, he made his way to the banister and descended the stairs. He was naked but for his socks, and he felt his lonely waddle brush back and forth between his thighs. He found his way downstairs to the liquor cabinet, and to the bottle of brandy.

"Turn on the lights," called Charlotte from the bedroom. "You'll fall."

He found the bottle of brandy easily enough but had to grope through several boxes to find a glass.

"Do you want your special glass?" Clark called over his shoulder. "Because I can't find it."

"No," Charlotte replied sleepily. "Any old glass."

Clark aimed the brandy into the glass, using his fingers to locate the stream. He stopped when the glass sounded full, more or less. It had begun to rain again that night, and the waterlogged wind threw itself against the windows and came through the cracks and chilled his bare buttocks. The hedges thrashed outside. There was no moon.

"Clark," called Charlotte above him.

He looked up. "Yes?"

"Is everything all right?"

"Of course," he said. "I'll be up in a minute, Charlie."

Her voice sounded small from upstairs. She said, "No, I mean, are *you* all right? How are you—How are you doing?" She paused. "Oh, I don't know. Do you want to talk? About anything. Your mother. Are you sad? I'll listen. I promise. Would you like that?"

He went to the foot of the stairs and stood there, head bent. He took a sip of the brandy and felt it slide down his throat.

"No," he said, shrugging. "I'm not sad. I don't want to talk."

"All right," she said. Again she paused. "So, I love you."

"Gee," said Clark. "Say that again?"

He rose one stair and listened for a moment, half-smiling, teething the rim of his glass.

"I don't like it when we yell across the house like this," Charlotte said after a moment.

"All right," Clark said. "I'll be up in a minute."

He stepped backward, felt around in the darkness of the foyer and came across a stool. He sat, legs slightly bent. He shuffled his stockinged feet back and forth a couple times and took slow sips.

After a while, he poured a little more brandy into the glass and looked around. The shadows played with the shadows. He did not yet feel quite right in the house. He didn't really know where anything was. He had expected to feel at home right away, kicking up his feet in the evenings. But nothing was anywhere yet. The dark trees rustled outside the window. He swirled the liquid in his glass.

Suddenly, he felt his heart surge forward desperately, like a dog in a sack, and he realized he wanted very much to talk. He lurched to the bottom of the stairs.

"Charlie?" he cried. "Charlie? You still awake?"

There was no response. He turned and looked back into the darkness. He had the definite impression of the darkness looking in on him. He wrapped himself in a blanket that hung over the armchair and sat on the bottom stair. After a while, he realized his muscles were rigid. It was almost as if he was waiting for somebody—the stranger, that shadow, that piece of darkness—to sidle up to him on the staircase and tell him the secret. He clutched the bottle by the neck. Throwing back his head, he licked the last drops of the thick liquid from his glass, and poured himself another.

FAMILY HAPPINESS

Several months into their uneasy living arrangement, Charlotte and her mother-in-law's dog were still not getting along. There seemed to be a dispute about which of them owned the new house. When Charlotte tried to fill his water dish, he snapped at her hand. In an effort to replicate a hunt, he would scatter his dog food and then go collect it again, and she often stepped on the food he'd forgotten about. Sometimes, when she was unpacking, the dog would come out of nowhere and snatch something out of a box and drag it to a corner and stand over it as if it were kill. It did not help in the least that Clark allowed the dog to sleep on the bed, a place he clearly took in his previous household, and she could feel his hostile shape on her legs all night. Every sunrise, when Tecumseh leapt off the bed and began to howl, Charlotte would shake her fist at him. The dog and the woman would stare at each other, his eyes white and hers dark. It was clear to both of them that they were vying with one another, just as Charlotte had vied with her mother-in-law when she was alive. With her dark eyes Charlotte would say, *This is my house*. With his defiant white eyes the dog would say, *There is no such thing as a house*.

But then, one spring morning, when Charlotte came to the door to fend off yet another fastidious request from Mr. Pitts, things changed. For Mr. Pitts, who lived at the crest of Quail Hollow Road and liked to stride up and down the hill in creased apple-green slacks nosing into everyone's business, was chastening Charlotte about the use of power tools as per the Clementine sound ordinance. Charlotte was doing her best to listen politely through the screen door. It was April, and yet out of all the people in the neighborhood, only Mr. Pitts had ever come to greet them. Although they had waved over the hedges at their neighbors the Ribbendrops, and on Saturday nights could hear the parties of the divorcee on the other side, in general no one in the neighborhood seemed to be taking Charlotte and Clark very seriously.

Except Mr. Pitts. How he went on and on! Charlotte was just about to raise her glove to interject, when she heard the strangest sound behind her. It was like the sound from a monster's throat. Before she knew it, Tecumseh was rising out of the shadow of the hall, leaping toward the old man's terrified face on the other side of the screen door, fangs bared and glinting.

The screen bowed with the dog's weight, and the old man stumbled backward. Charlotte put her hand to her face. She didn't even have time to apologize. The man was hightailing it back up the hill. And he never bothered them again.

After that, Charlotte and Tecumseh got along rather well. Theirs was more of a truce than a friendship. Charlotte did not snuggle or woo him, like Clark did. She would sometimes pat him on the head, right where the lobes of his brain left a soft recess. In a gesture of compromise, the dog accepted his new bed downstairs underneath the liquor cabinet, and Charlotte got up dutifully at first howl, to let him go outside to greet the sun god or whatever it was he did. It occurred to Charlotte that the truce she was making was also with the dead woman who, in their years together, had never once been kind to her.

How had it come and gone so quickly? One minute she was watching a tall, curly-headed stranger chase his scattered newspaper down the street, and she was laughing—for what she remembered first was the sound of her own laughter, an egg breaking in her chest—and eleven ardent weeks later, they were married. During those eleven weeks, Clark had told Charlotte all about his parents—rapturous stories of how they had built churches by candlelight in Mexico, how his mother as a young woman had once taken part in a certain Latin American revolution by delivering a cake with a secret map in it. The way Clark spoke, one couldn't help but imagine the young couple running over the stones of the world in high boots—brave, semi-divine. She wanted in to a family like that.

For she, on the other hand, had been adopted at the age of two by an aging couple by the name of Paul and Dodie Gagliardo, who lived in a nearby industrial town once famous for its production of panty hose. She remembered little of note from her childhood: a ubiquity of graham crackers, an inability to bounce a ball, the battlement-like shape of the mill buildings at dusk, cold window panes. She did not know or want to know what had become of her birth mother, although there remained snatches of memories, and those snatches of memories felt like little stabs when they surfaced, and left her with no whole, and she might as well have beaten herself on the head with an adze if she was going to spend her life speculating about it. *Why why why*. Well, why not? It wasn't a big mystery. Some people just don't want children. She understood that. She herself, for example, was sometimes frightened of them, frightened especially when holding babies—how they swayed about searching for the pretty colors.

Paul and Dodie Gagliardo were schoolteachers with pleasant, tea-colored faces made somewhat tense over time by their inability to conceive. Charlotte attended the school at which Daddy Gagliardo taught science, and he often walked her home from school, pointing out the early evening stars that shone over the brick horizon of the mill buildings. They had all done quite well together, and as far as one could measure, there was love. Love of the undemonstrative, old-world stripe—the love that bakes bread, that paws at the face with a spit-dampened Kleenex. But it was the cordial estrangement between them all in later years—just the blameless, gradual drifting apart—that was most real, reinforcing the fact that they had never technically belonged to one another, most especially not to Charlotte.

She had been ashamed to tell Clark about the true nature of her relationship with the Gagliardos. When she finally confessed, of all things, he laughed. He covered his face with his hands. "I was so confused," he laughed. "Charlotte Gagliardo! You didn't *look* Italian." And that was that. No shame, no coldness, no backing away. Only this gentle bemusement, for wasn't life tricky? If she had said, I was born of a clam, he would have said, I'd like to hear about *that*!

What he taught her then, with his strangely trusting, hell-bent love was, if life was tricky, you were freed from the burden of having to play it straight yourself, and anything was possible—anything. You could spend entire afternoons floating in inner tubes, you could commandeer the megaphone from the Bingo leader at the boardwalk, you could get engaged, you could talk with relative impunity about the fantastic plans you would never enact, you could drive up to your parent's house unannounced, holding the hand of a woman almost as tall and thin as you, she shyly folding a strand of stiff blonde hair behind her ear, and you could say, This is Charlotte. We just got married.

But of course, impulsive romantic gestures are not universally admired. Vera Adair had slumped perceptibly when she met Charlotte, holding out a limp hand, and saying to her son, Some smile she's got. At that point Charlotte felt Clark cringe beside her, for the crookedness of her eyeteeth was a sore point he well knew, ever since they had called her Chops at school. Charlotte clapped a hand over her mouth. And just then, a towering man in a wool sweater who was Clark's father emerged from his study and took Charlotte by the arm into a sitting room and offered her a drink in congratulations.

And that's the way the visits went for two years. Toward the end of her life, the strange, impulsive woman became more withdrawn, her stories more fantastical, but she never quite gave up taunting Charlotte with her particular intolerance for rejection and surprise. It was almost as if she were prodding Charlotte with whom she no longer wished to be—a loner, a skeptic, an orphan—slumming in the realms of family happiness. More than once, on visits, Charlotte had found her own suitcase packed prematurely by the door, or a taxi mysteriously waiting on the street, and Vera would chirp from a distant room, dressed in her signature white nightgown, "Oh, I thought you were *leaving* today, dear."

Suddenly, the quality of this memory made Charlotte laugh. Across from her, at the kitchen table, Clark looked up from his crossword puzzle. The dog sat beside them on the linoleum floor, watching the toast as Charlotte lifted it off the plate. His lips were caught inside his mouth. Charlotte laughed again but more tenderly, and she reached out and pat the dog on the head.

"What's so funny?" said Clark. "Why do you keep chuckling to yourself?"

Charlotte fed the dog her toast, which he ate in large, crocodile bites.

"Oh," she said, dusting off her hands, looking around at the house, which was finally starting to look like a real, lived-in house. "I'm just proud of us. How we've all—gone forward so normally. All things considered. The past, I mean. The crazy past."

Clark closed his naked legs and opened them again. He was in his underwear, holding a blue crayon.

"Sure," he said.

"Even the dog," said Charlotte. "I think he's completely recovered. *Voila*. A fresh start."

She smiled down at the animal, who had swallowed his treat and was looking up at his new mistress—history, a rumor.

END OF DISCUSSION

By the time summer came, the Adairs were doing quite well. They passed many dexterous nights in bed, and stayed up late drinking root beer or brandy in the darkness, laughing and playing Pick It Up Now and various other games they'd invented in their married, childless idleness. It felt to them both that perhaps it was now, perhaps now life was starting up, for real, at last. They opened all the windows and summer air filled the house. The rooms were painted, the furniture largely in place. Tecumseh continued to scatter and hunt for his dog food, but he didn't howl at sunrise much. And after the doghouse was built in the backyard, Charlotte often checked to make sure he had not choked himself by encircling the structure with his chain. As for Clark, he had not seen the feminine shadow again, and he never thought of it.

Charlotte had found herself a hopefully very temporary job as a secretary for a cheerful negligence lawyer named Warren Ziff, and Clark, who had just completed his first term at Clementine Junior High, was relieved to have the summer off. Finally, he didn't have to coddle or interrogate anybody for masturbating in the bathrooms or for defacing the teacher's lounge or for handcuffing somebody else to a shower stall, for everything kids did that was transgressive and passionate and senseless—for everything kids did, really. He didn't have to coddle the teachers, who bickered and complained and puked about everything. He hated listening to people. He was awful at it. Well, he was all right at listening, but then people wanted to know what you thought. People wanted to know whose side you came down on. Take this, for example: two boys get in trouble for fighting. The first boy says the second started it, the second says the first, and they've both got black eyes. Well, if they've both got black eyes, what's the problem?

There was something wild in children, he thought sometimes, but you could not love that wildness and it was not particularly beautiful. You could only hold it at bay until it died by itself.

Clark was supposed to be taking night classes. He had his teaching certificate, but officially he wasn't trained to be a guidance counselor. He wasn't certified. In a pinch, when the previous guidance counselor had been struck with some obscure joint disease, the junior high school had hired Clark on the condition that he finish his qualifications by taking human development classes at the Clementine Community College. But over time, the night classes bored Clark and he stopped going. He figured humans would continue to develop whether or not he took classes about them. And the trick to guiding a child? Get the hell out of the way. You need a certificate for that?

Clark liked summer vacation and he took it very seriously. He liked being a guidance counselor in the summers. He slept late in the warm mornings, and when it started to get cool again he would know it was evening and would begin to make dinner for Charlotte, stirring a pot, opening a beer, watching TV, watching the light change. He liked the soberness of shadows, long and thin like him. By day, he walked Tecumseh around the neighborhood. He felt that he and the dog understood one another. Sometimes Clark took him to the apple orchard across the street and let him bark at the blackbirds. Together, they sat on the brittle grass in the shade, the husky's tongue lolling out on the side, dreaming of different things.

Then one day, Clark slipped while chaining Tecumseh to his doghouse. After a split second, in which dog and man were mutually surprised, the dog bounded off with such energy that it was clear he had been eagerly awaiting the opportunity. Clark was temporarily paralyzed by the revelation that the dog did not feel indebted to him at all, that love was not a certain byproduct of two beings sticking it out through time. He shouted after the dog, but Tecumseh only looked back once before pushing through the hedges and his look asked, *Why did you try to keep me, when there is nothing that stays?*

Clark combed the neighborhood all day, calling for him. *Tecumseh! Tecuhhhhmseh!*

He was irate with himself. How could he have bungled this, his one final responsibility to his mother? Perhaps he should not have kept the dog; perhaps it was not what she would have wanted. Now he had to keep swatting her disappointed face from his mind. He did not enjoy remembering her anyway except in his earliest memories, when she was a gorgeous and exotic young woman in Carnifex Ferry and he her cherubim, her favorite, her favorite by leagues, strolling around ponds together making fun of the frogs, botanizing together in the damp woods behind the house, staying home from school sometimes. He could even remember as far back to sleeping on her breast, he could remember that primitively. It made him feel like a good son not to remember her after she started to become . . . well, strange. She had been strange for as long as he could remember, but strange in a marvelous way, a child's way. A circus, a smear of pinwheels. But then something happened. He grew up? The memory of her eyes those final years, dark and detached and accusing, how her body almost smoldered with misery, he refused it. She had ended her life. This was a point she was making. She had pointedly ended the discussion.

In bed that night, Charlotte touched her husband's arm.

"He'll come back," she said. "The dog will come back."

"Charlotte," Clark said. "If you were chained to a post all day, then you escaped, would you come back?"

She chewed the side of her cheek. "Well. Being chained to a post has its pros and cons."

"Oh God, who knows," Clark said, sighing. "Maybe he's on a quest. Maybe . . . maybe he's gone looking for someone. Maybe he's gone looking for my mother."

Charlotte squirmed. She had grown attached to the dog, and the sudden recognition of this was unpleasant to her.

"Get real," she said, gritting her teeth. "He's just a dog. He'll take anybody. He doesn't know love from rawhide."

Clark looked at her with empty eyes. "Well, then," he murmured, "maybe he's angry. Maybe he thinks we're not good people."

"Ridiculous. A dog can't get angry. A dog can't hold a grudge."

"Don't be so sure. Everything in the whole world has a memory. The land has a memory. Didn't you ever think about what a fossil is? And what about the rings in a tree? Try flying in a plane—"

"I've flown in a *plane*."

"—and you can see scars in the vegetation, from where there were fires, and nothing grows there. In memoriam. Out of respect. The Indians," he continued, wagging his finger, "they thought you kept your body in the afterlife. They used to cut their signatures into their victims' bodies so that the victims would remember who killed them once they were dead."

Clark turned on his side and stared out at the moon. The moon was low. It looked burdened, and its face was pocked with craters. Suddenly he felt very angry. The china was gone, and now the dog. All he had left of his mother were some keys and a hairbrush and a couple of unpleasant images. After a moment, the grip the anger had on his throat relaxed, and left him with a smaller, bitterer thing. He thought of his mother and Charlotte bickering, in distant rooms of memories.

"Besides," he said, "*you* ought to know about grudges."

He turned heavily on the bed, facing away. And then, as if alerted to the very moods of his heart, the shadow crossed the doorway again, carrying a wine glass.

He sat up.

Charlotte's back was turned away from him, toward the window. He looked beyond her at the tree trunks out the window, womanish in shape. Had the figure been a very realistic illusion cast across the room by headlights?

"Oh, Jesus," he said.

He lay back down.

"What," said Charlotte. "What is it now?"

Then an enormous fatigue overcame him, and suddenly he did not care to understand anything. He did not even care if a real woman had strolled past his bedroom door. It did not matter. He felt enormously tired, asked for one thing too many.

"I don't know," he said. "It's nothing. Go back to sleep."

A SPECIAL ARRANGEMENT

The summer in Clementine grew hot and gusty. The wind at night kept Clark awake, and husband and wife traded shifts of sleeplessness, grousing in sleepy talk about the smallness of the bed and the length of Clark's limbs. The superficiality of sleep was making Clark's dreams more vivid to him—thunderstorms, the thunderstorms at Carnifex Ferry, the shaking of God's great cookie sheet over his boyhood. And when he awoke late in the darkness, he could not resist staring at the doorway. He began to believe it would only be a matter of time—days, minutes—before he'd be confronted again by the impossible shape. He watched Charlotte's lovely back in the darkness. If he were to wake her, what would he say?

The summer had grown so hot that Clark had taken to spending his days at the local swimming pool. He spent the long days wading through the cool blue water among children and housewives and old, chicken-armed men, and then retreating, temporarily refreshed, to his chair on the grass. In the summer heat, the walk to the pool almost killed him, making the vision of the pool all the more Elysian. He was reminded, unpleasantly, that certain animals come to the water to die.

But it was so *hot*. Even the sky was parched. It had not rained in weeks. Only sitting there on the poolside grass, turning brown and watching the kids play, did Clark feel relieved from both the heat and the fear. He felt normal and refreshed and not at all bothered by shadows. It was good to get out of the house. If you immersed yourself in normal American pastimes, he found, you could quite easily reap the benefits of normality. No one was asking you to be a visionary.

Besides, he liked to watch the kids play. They gave him energy, in an abstract sense. He liked kids a great deal, though he did not like guiding them. He liked childhood. Before everything. He liked to watch kids be kids, bellyflopping off the low dive, falling down violently like big branches, without the remotest regard for their own well-being. He liked to see them running around shivering and picking shamelessly at their crotches, their heads slick like seals, and sometimes it took a lot of effort for him not to run out and join them but to stay in the sun, baking himself into a palsy along with the other adults, whose large hips and hairy paunches made them appear, sprawled across the poolside grass, like slaughtered buffalo.

Clark propped a leg up on the lounge chair and gazed out through his sunglasses. It was Free Swim, and the kids in the pool were performing for him. He laughed and clapped. They liked having his attention. He was good with kids, and had very recently felt a yearning for one of his own. Some of the kids seemed to know him from school and bumped into each other getting in line. Smiling at him, one of them ran down the board and sailed out over the water in consummate flop position, his face making a wet slap against the surface. The flop was so perfect that when the boy emerged from the pool he staggered over to his mother, trying not to cry.

The mother, a pretty young brunette with chunky shoulders that glistened with baby oil, comforted the boy in her arms. Clark watched them, as the boy fell magically to sleep against her. There was something heroic about parenthood, Clark thought. It made heroes out of people, ordinary people, tax accountants and dental assistants and even flawed, crazy people. Such people were always in the paper, saving their children from runaway buses and threshing machines, putting their bodies in harm's way, developing superhuman strength and acuity. So much did their children rely on them that they became everyday gods, emerging from a cloud of baking flour, an umbrella for a staff.

He and Charlotte weren't going to have any children. She didn't want any. Before their marriage, she had stated this very clearly as a precondition. She said it was entirely too easy to be a wretched parent, and then had laughed lightly, saying, Look at us. Clark agreed. He said of course he didn't want any either and also laughed, and buried his nose in her hair.

But the truth was he hadn't thought about it at all. He had wanted to get married to Charlotte so badly that when he looked at her, she was the only thing he saw. His parents' marriage was in shambles by then, thanks to Mrs. Flanigan, his sister Mary had moved to Detroit with her husband, Jerome, and had washed her hands of them, and his mother was changing into a woman he barely recognized. Charlotte was the one vibrant thing in the world. She crackled. She glowed. She made the most fascinating fusses. He loved her light touch, her diffidence, the way she walked ahead without waiting, he loved the damp silk blouse she wore one evening to a summer concert and the very shoots of grass that she wore unknowingly in her pale yellow hair. He even loved her mysterious origins, because it reinforced his suspicion that he had a princess on his hands. Everything else fell away. She had a lean, untrammeled, hitchless body. It ran in milk rivers to the ground. And now he knew they could be happy and they could live well. They could be well and happy, but maybe they would never be heroes.

Clark leaned back and shut his eyes. He felt a prick of pain in his heart, but smiled anyway. Up at the sun he smiled. He heard the thump of a ball being volleyed, and the register bell at the snack bar and the chanting of a group of girls sitting nearby, a soft patty cake, *You said I said he said so. He said you said I said no. One for the east. One for the west. One for the one that I love best.* Soon, these sounds became distant and all he heard, between the distant, sea-sound of his blood, was his heartbeat.

A cold hand touched his shoulder.

"Hey," a voice was saying. "Hey. Excuse me."

Clark opened his eyes to see a teenage girl wearing gigantic sunglasses.

"Hello," he said.

"Hello," she said. "You're Mr. Adair, right? You were my guidance counselor last year." Clark tried to focus on her, but she split into six identical teenage girls.

She raised her sunglasses. "It's Judy."

"Oh, hey, Judy," he lied. "How's your summer going?"

"Pretty good. I don't belong to this pool but today I'm a guest. My kid brother has a friend who's a member." She lowered her glasses and surveyed the pool. Her hair was dark and coarse, and she wore a sagging pink swimsuit with a black sash. He didn't remember her whatsoever. She must have been all right. He only remembered the lost and troubled ones, the medicated ones, the ones he had to send away to St. Luke's. He looked back up at the girl. Judy, he thought, Judy . . . Suddenly, he felt utterly confused.

"Listen," the girl said, "it's none of my business, but you've been sleeping out here in the sun for hours. You're red as a lobster. I thought maybe you should move into the shade."

Clark looked at the sky, and indeed, the sun was much further west. Surrounding him, the grass was almost empty, but for two rumpled towels. He stood up quickly, and his vision filled with blackness.

"Are you okay?" Judy asked.

"I'm completely fine," said Clark, falling back blind into his chair.

The girl trotted off toward the snack bar and gestured for service. Clark edged his way poolside and stood transfixed by the faint, shimmering, chemical blueness.

"Whoa," said Judy, coming up out of nowhere. She led him back to his chair and put a cup of water in his hands. "No swimmy swim for you yet. Drink this first. Besides, you shouldn't go in there during Free Swim. Wait for Adult Swim. It's chaos during Free Swim. I'm surprised there aren't more fatalities."

She stood and watched him until he finished drinking.

"Thanks," he said. But he didn't feel any better.

They sat quietly for several moments. Clark hoped she wasn't looking for some guidance. Then he wondered if he should be chatting with her socially at all, what the rules were about that. Then he wondered if she was real or if she was a shadow. He swung his heavy head in her direction and gave her a sideways look. He slapped the arms of his beach chair with finality.

But Judy said, "Listen." She reached into her sash and took out a tightly folded piece of paper. "This your dog?"

Clark started. He pointed to the poster he'd stapled to telephone polls all around town. "Tecumseh!"

"Yeah," she said. "Gray dog? Big paws?"

"Yes," he said, though all of this was obvious in the photograph.

"I think I know where he is," said Judy. "But don't get excited. I can't promise. It's just I've got a knack for these things. I take down every lost pet poster I see. It's kind of a side business. Sometimes they give rewards and things."

"Oh," said Clark. "Sure. We'll give a reward."

Judy leaned back. "Oh, no, I couldn't take money from you, Mr. Adair, not after how much you helped me out in school last year."

Clark smiled, nodding, though his head felt like hot pudding and he had no bloody idea what she was talking about. He was starting to feel slightly panicked.

"I do have one itty-bitty thing to ask of you," said Judy, pushing her sunglasses up with one finger. She turned and gestured up the hill, where a small boy was hugging a volleyball to his chest. "You see that kid up there on the volleyball court? Little guy, with glasses?"

Clark looked up the hill.

"His name is James. He's my kid brother. He's a good little guy. *Very* smart. I'd say—and I can say this word without cheapening it?—genius."

"Mm," said Clark.

"He's small for his age. All the nutrients go straight to his brain. But, you know, so what if he can't swim? So what if he can't do a pull-up? Could Einstein swim? Could Amerigo Vespucci do a pull-up?"

Just then, the lifeguard—a skinny immigrant named Gundars who had an impenetrable accent and who wore his regulation red windbreaker zipped to the throat—blew his whistle. Everyone stopped and looked up at him, wondering if they were going to be able to understand what he had to say. Gundars shifted in his chair, cleared his throat. Then he cried, "Adult Svim!"

The children moaned. They rubbed their eyes, and pulled themselves out of the pool. Meanwhile, several corpulent adults rolled into the pool like great fleshy hulls and began to swim laps. A group of young mothers tread in the deep end talking, their bright bathing caps like a basket of colored eggs.

Judy cleared her throat. "Well, anyway," she continued, "James is small for his age. You wouldn't know it, but he's going to Clementine Junior High next fall, where you work." Then she added, with sudden heartiness, "Isn't that *great*?" She spoke in a stagy, unnatural way, as if she were reading from enormous cue cards above Clark's head.

"Yes," said Clark. "That's great."

Clark looked at the probing blue of the pool and felt an almost rapacious desire for it. It swung back and forth in his vision like a portrait on a hook. Licking his lips, he imagined the chilliness of the deep end against his burnt skin.

"I need to ask you a favor," the girl said. She put her hand on his arm, and its coldness shocked him and caused him to look down at her. She took off her sunglasses, revealing large, oil-dark eyes with discolored circles underneath, the fatigued eyes of an adult. "See, sometimes he gets picked on. In fact, he gets picked on all the time. I'll be up at the high school. I won't be able to keep an eye on him this year. Could you? Could you guide him, as you so kindly did for me?"

Clark looked up at the volleyball court, where a pack of older boys were moving toward the unnaturally small kid, gesturing for the volleyball. Instead of forking it over, the boy clutched it to his chest. One by one, the older boys took off their baseball caps and began swatting James in the head with them.

"All right," said Clark. "You know, it's my job anyway."

"No," said Judy. "It needs to be more than that. A special arrangement."

"Yes, yes," said Clark, heading off in something of a stagger toward the low dive, "I promise already."

"Thank you," Judy said, beaming. She waved the poster at him. "A promise is a promise!" Then she began scrambling the hill, toward her brother. She stopped several paces off. "Don't forget his name," she called over her shoulder, "James. James Nye!"

Clark waved and nodded and then turned his attention to the pool. He stuck his toe in the water. It was cool and anesthetizingly, tropically blue. Once he got in, he was going to drink the whole damn thing.

He smiled at the women treading nearby, and then found himself climbing the rings to the diving board. Walking out on its rough tongue, the reverberations rushed up his body, and in the refracted water below the women smiled, cheeks illuminated, kicking like cherubs stuck in smog. He bounced once, twice. He felt his flesh sag and spring back up. And when he jumped, he was acutely aware of the feeling of weightlessness, of nothing. For it was this sensation he'd been feeling since their arrival at 12 Quail Hollow Road, a feeling of not rising and not falling, a feeling of not being quite oneself, of not quite being.

BARBECUE

"And this," Charlotte turned to him, indicating him with her palm, "is my wonderful husband, Clark."

The old couple looked up and squinted. Clark folded his arms and unfolded them. They were burnt the color of mangos, as was his forehead. He had brushed his hair back with pomade because the slightest touch hurt his sunburn.

"You're too tall to see," said the old man. His eyeglasses were smudged. "And where do you live, Clark?"

"The Lippet's old house!" yelled the old man's wife before Clark could answer. "They said that already. That's where they *live*. They just moved in this winter. Where Bob and Marion Lippet used to live."

Clark leaned forward, careful not to touch himself anywhere. "The Lippets?" he said. "What were they like?"

The old woman looked up at him and waited for his question to float down to her. A cloud of barbecue smoke wafted over to them and then out of the gate through which Clark and Charlotte had recently entered. A crowd of about twenty-five decent-looking people milled on the perfect grass beyond.

Charlotte had been overjoyed to discover the very impersonal Xeroxed invitation to the barbecue stuffed into their mailbox. They hadn't yet been invited to anything in the neighborhood. Meanwhile, Clark had looked at the hill up which he would soon be forced to march, his sunburned skin smarting all over, and he felt with sudden conviction that going to a neighborhood barbecue would be cruel and unusual. He didn't want to meet anybody. He didn't feel like meeting anybody. If you were meant to meet people, you'd meet them by chance, in the rain. But she had looked so excited, and he could never resist any girlish expression on her part. And of course, it was sort of lonely to be the New People, lost in your own neighborhood.

"Bob and Marion Lippet," said the old lady. "He was some sort of a chemist and she taught music. Very nice young couple. We were all so sad when they left. It was rather sudden. They left without a word. Just drove away. Nobody knows where they went."

"Just like the ones before them," said the old man. "The ones always fighting. You could hear them in the summertime."

"No need to talk about all that," said the woman. "Pure coincidence."

"And the ones before *them*," said the man. "A coincidence too? Makes you wonder."

Clark cocked his head. "What?" he said.

"Now, Marion Lippet," said the old man, "was a nurse."

"Marion Lippet was a music teacher," said his wife. "She always carried rosin in her skirt pocket."

"Marion Lippet was a nurse," said the old man. "I'm sure of it."

Clark looked back and forth at them.

"Marion Lippet was a music teacher," said the old lady. "They had a baby grand in the living room. You could hear the music all afternoon. Child's music. Practicing scales. "*Für Elise,*' 'The March of the Woodchucks.' Always children around but none of their own."

"Marion Lippet was barren," said the old man.

"Bob Lippet was a burn victim," said the old woman. "He was very handsome in an Irish way. A broad, intelligent forehead and shining blue eyes. But he'd been in a terrible fire as a child, and his body was covered with scars to the neck. It looked almost as if he was wearing a suit of them. He wore gloves sometimes so as not to scare the children when they came for lessons with Marion."

"Marion drank a bit."

"Marion drank an awful lot. But never were there two more charming people. God knows if you scratch anyone deep enough . . ."

"The Fiorellos!" cried the old man. "*That* was the name of the couple before. Ran away too!"

"All right already," said his wife. "Enough of that."

The old lady smiled up at Clark.

Clark looked back at the old couple, and after a moment he smiled back. To his surprise, he was actually enjoying the barbecue. He was enjoying hearing about the Lippets. He liked them. Suddenly, they were very real to him and he liked them. He pictured Bob walking around the house, pensively rubbing ointment on his arms. He pictured barren Marion swaying to music in some gauzy, sun-illuminated dress. And then they left, in a mysterious flourish, leaving hairpins on the floor and music fading in the rafters. Clark got the sense, now that he thought of it, of music left behind. And as Charlotte looped her arm through his, he also remembered the feminine shadow crossing the door. *Makes you wonder.*

"Well," said Charlotte, who had not been listening. "I guess I'll go get a hamburger or something." She was gazing into the yard at the people. A child ran by holding a lit sparkler. A young, glossy-haired woman lurched after him a couple steps and said, "Remember it's not for eating, Freddie." The woman smiled, drew her hair back from her eyes, sighed, and walked after the child.

"Would you like to come, Clark?" said Charlotte. "And meet some more neighbors? I'd sure like to get to know some more of our neighbors."

"No," said Clark, smiling down at the old couple. "I'll stay right here with . . ."

"Edith and Stan."

"Oh," Charlotte said. "All right." She bent down toward the old man. "Which ones are the Girgises?"

The old man indicated the host couple, who were standing by the grill, dressed in bold primary colors. In fact, it was the comely Mrs. Girgis who'd walked past in a shower-fresh cloud just a moment earlier, and seeing her swinging hair filled Charlotte with a spoony feeling. She was just the sort of girl that other girls would have found desirable in the school yard, the sort of girl Charlotte would not have been able to win the heart of back then, as Chops. Briefly, she indulged the image of the two of them throwing apples at each other in the orchard. She left Clark at the periphery and went to introduce herself. For this was the neighborhood she had once dreamed of, now miraculously delivered on a platter of grass. This was the safety, the belonging, the boring beauty. This was the wagon circle. A haven inscribed by the smell of creosote and bug spray.

Smiling, the breeze on her bare arms, Charlotte crossed the yard. Somehow, despite all this—the breeze, the creosote—she was fleetingly troubled by the sense that she was walking up to the front of a classroom. Walking up to take the pointer from Mrs. Lines, who stood before the map of the world. Where was Oman, after all? She still didn't know. And was the teacher's name really Mrs. Lines, or was the name merely an association with all those red hash marks on paper, all those shameful errors? The sight of a corrected paper used to make Charlotte dizzy. *They know*, she would think. They have now seen the flaws that made me what I am, ugly even to my own mother.

Then just as suddenly, her hand was holding the fine-boned hand of a smiling Meg Girgis, who was pulling her forward and out, back into the circle. A sandy-haired man emerged from a cloud of smoke, a child on his hip. Mrs. Lines shrank back into a whisper, and soon Charlotte and her hosts were laughing like old friends. Meg Girgis, raven-haired and tennisy looking, detached the child from her husband's hip, and set him down in the grass.

"And did your husband come along, Charlotte? Is he that tall fellow over with Stan and Edith?"

"Yes he is," said Charlotte, turning and waving. "Clark!"

Clark did not hear. He was still talking to the old couple by the fence, who were stretching up on their toes to listen to him. Charlotte cleared her throat.

"Clark!" she called again. She turned back. "Oh well," she said.

"And do you two have any children, Charlotte?" asked Meg.

"Lord, no," said Charlotte. Then, shaking her head rapidly, "Not yet, I mean."

Meg turned to her husband. "Charlotte and Clark just moved into the Lippets' old house."

"*Oh*," said Glen. His face took on a concerned, probing look. "How's it going? Everything OK?"

"Oh great," said Charlotte. "Just great."

"Well, we were hoping you'd come," said Meg gently.

"Of course we'd come," said Charlotte. "We don't know anybody at all in town. We don't know a soul. We just sit around and stare at each other. It's like we live in a little diorama or something. Help, help! Let us out!"

Meg and Glen smiled but did not laugh. They were very nice people. Charlotte turned around and tried to get Clark's attention again, but he was still absorbed in his conversation with the old couple. In fact, the old couple were leaning toward him with expressions of almost desperate intensity. Charlotte felt a shudder run up her body.

"Wow," Meg said. "He must be very interesting, your Clark."

"He is," said Charlotte. "I wonder what he's yakking about. I'll just go and get him. I'd like him to meet you."

As she recrossed the perfect Girgesian grass, she watched her husband's hands gesturing in the dusk. When she reached them, she tugged on his shirtsleeve and was about to ask him to excuse himself when she stopped short. The old couple's mouths were open. Their eyes rolled toward her vacantly. The old man's glasses slid to the end of his nose. Clark straightened and scratched his cheek.

"I was just telling Edith and Stan a story," he said.

The old woman clutched Charlotte on the elbow, and put one hand over her heart.

"I can't believe it," she whispered. "I can't believe he escaped with his *life*!"

The man drew a long breath. "To put the map inside a *cake*. Who would have thought of it?"

"Of what?" said Charlotte.

"The Revolution!" bellowed the man, pushing out his chest. Several of the guests turned to look. "When your husband saved the Revolution from defeat!"

Clark scratched his cheek again.

"Please. Please go on," begged the woman. "You were leaving the jail after giving the general the cake . . ."

"What general?" laughed Charlotte. "What cake?"

Standing there, Charlotte felt dizzy. The *Revolution*! Of course. She looked around, as if she might see Vera herself stride out of the rhododendron, dusting off her hands, saying, *Let me tell it!* The story was one of her classics, one of her fantasies! And now Clark had rewritten it with himself as the hero? Charlotte drew the back of her wrist across her forehead. Suddenly the sky and the air seemed too close—a small box she was shut in.

Just then, Meg Girgis flounced off the porch and begin to walk across the yard toward the group of them, perfect tan knees moving underneath her plastic apron. Her approach made Charlotte freeze; she could never be friends with a woman like that.

She spun around to collide with the body of her husband, his sunburnt skin making him only vaguely familiar, his eyes astral blue. The sky slid around like jelly behind him.

"Let's *go*," Charlotte said. The old couple protested and reached after them as they passed hurriedly through the gate and disappeared back down the hill, to where the Lippets used to live.

EXTRAVAGANCE

"You don't like it?" Clark said. "I got a very good deal on it."

Charlotte stood over the gleaming machine with a blank expression on her face. She blinked twice, her brow furrowing. She had just come home from work. The summer sky behind her was deepening. She removed her pumps and stood in the yard without responding.

Clark looked over at her. "I got a very good deal on it, I said. End of summer closeout."

"I don't want to know how much," she said.

"Guess how much."

"I don't want to guess. I don't like to guess. Let's not turn this into a thing. I don't care. I want to go inside where there's no bugs."

"Three hundred dollars," he said, and Charlotte flinched at the number, closing her eyes. "It was advertised for twice that. Look," he patted the saddle, "power steering, four-wheel drive. I could take this out on the freeway."

"I want to have a gin and tonic," she said. "I want to sit inside and drink it where there's no bugs."

"And look," he said, catching her wrist and dragging her around the other side. "Stainless steel body, fenders, just like a car. Oh, and a self-contained removal system. See, the grass gets chewed up there under the rotor," he pointed vaguely underneath the little tractor, "and then it comes through this pipe here, and gets shunted into this sack back here, which has a little chute on the bottom, and if you raise it . . ." he struggled to move the arm, his T-shirt sliding up over his back. "If you raise it . . ."

Charlotte turned and went inside.

He came after her in the kitchen.

"You don't like it," he said.

"We don't need it," she said. "It's an extravagance."

"Well, if you look at it that way, we don't really need that oven. We don't need chairs or beds or indoor plumbing. Hell, we don't even need this damn house. A house is an extravagance. We could live under the stars, like antelope."

Charlotte was holding her special glass with nothing in it. He stood between her and the freezer.

"I can return it, if you absolutely hate it," said Clark. "If you *really* want me to."

"I'd like some ice, please," said Charlotte.

"How extravagant of you." He stepped aside.

"So you disapprove," he said.

She moved past him, took several frostbitten ice cubes from the tray and placed them in the glass. She poured herself some gin, screwed the cap on hard, and looked at him.

"What the hell is *wrong* with you these days?" she said.

"What," he said. "With me?"

"You've been behaving so strangely. You walk around in a daze. You pace around at night. You do strange things." She looked down into her glass. "I don't feel you're really here."

"I'm right here!" Clark laughed expansively.

"But what are you *thinking*?" she said. She pointed at him with her gin. "A sit-down mower? A baby pool? Last week, you bought a baby pool, Clark."

"Yes?" he said, waiting.

"Is it—is it for yourself?"

"I sit in it. I cool off in it, it's so damned hot in this town."

"But you cool off at the *pool*," she said. "You go to the pool every day. All you do is go to the pool and eat your mayonnaise sandwiches. I've been wanting to ask you about *those* for weeks. It's weird." She switched her glass from one hand to the other. "I mean, I'd like to understand. Are they something—are they something your—" she looked down again into her glass, "—your mother used to make for you? Is this some way of—of dealing with her absence? Is this some kind of 'reenactment'?"

"Ha," said Clark. "Where are you getting these words?"

"From the books by your bed. For your night class."

"Those are aca*dem*ic words, Charlotte. They're not for people."

She looked at him for a long moment.

"You lied to those old people," she said. "At the barbecue."

"Good grief. Not this again."

"Why did you lie to them, Clark? I don't understand."

"I was bored. I was bored! I'm bored right now just thinking about that stupid picnic. All the stupid things. Barbecues.

Housework. Painting. Dusting. Parent–teacher conferences. It's *busy*work. It's dreck. It's *unimaginative*."

"But it's life!" cried Charlotte. "Your life. It's a *nice* life."

He walked around in a small circle and came back to where he'd been standing.

"Are we done with this subject?" he said.

"What about when they find out you were lying? What will people think of you?"

"To hell with when they find out," Clark said. "It was funny. It was a joke. It was for fun."

"But it was a lie. A fantasy. You understand that, right?" Charlotte touched him on the hand, but he moved his hand.

"Of course I understand that," he said, tugging at the collar of his T-shirt. "I didn't mean to upset the exquisite balance of the universe."

"Stop," Charlotte said. Her eyes were glassy. "We never used to talk like this. Did we? Sometimes these days I don't recognize you. Not since we moved in here. Don't you feel it too? A strangeness."

She put out her hand and Clark moved just out of reach. He looked across the counter at her, and gestured at her glass.

"Have about six more of those rickeys of yours and everything will be just fine." He laughed harshly. "And quit being so Christly, Charlotte. What, you never lied? You didn't even tell me your big secret until we were already engaged. You remember? For the longest time, you let me go around thinking you were the natural daughter of two elderly Italians. That's a pretty big lie, isn't it? I was pretty damned confused by that myself."

Now Charlotte stepped back. Her expression was that of such disappointment that Clark felt a twitch in his hand as if he wanted to strike his own face. She held the glass of gin limply in her hand, and some of it dripped onto the linoleum floor. Without another word, she turned and disappeared into the dark living room.

Clark stood with his hands open as one falsely accused of stealing. Around him, the appliances hummed in disuse. He leaned against the counter, rubbing his head. So what if she was right. He had been feeling strange. Tired. Immobilized. Surrounded on all sides, as if he was living in a ditch. For several weeks now, he hadn't once slept through the night. Fatigued throughout the day, simple things had become difficult, and the truth about the mayonnaise sandwiches was that they were the easiest things to make.

Worse than all that, his reasoning was compromised, his ability to tell something real from something imagined. He thought of the feminine shape he'd seen cross the bedroom doorway, and how he decided it was a shadow from the trees. But since then, he'd heard murmured words in the pantry, a flash of a naked thigh in the guest bedroom that dissolved upon second look. Recently, he'd been awoken in the night by what he thought was a man blowing his nose, but when he listened, there was nothing. How could he tell Charlotte, queen of reason, who would only think him crazy? And *was he*? He threw a dishrag into the sink.

"Damn it," he said to the empty room.

He looked out at the lawn mower in the backyard. It was an extravagance. He tried to think of what had compelled him to go and buy it in the first place. He had intended to go and do something helpful, to buy a spade or some marigold seeds for Charlotte's theoretical garden. The salesman had shown him the mower instead. There was a certain scent that new machinery gave off. It smelled of promise and of industry. At one point in his boyhood, he had seen, with his father, a series of freshly assembled cars come out of their hangars on rolling treads, each one shinier than the next. When he saw the mower and he saw himself on its saddle, he thought, aren't I that man, the sort of man for whom such inventions are made?

"Charlie?" he called into the dark living room. "You there?"

She did not respond, but he heard her breathing. He heard her teeth against the glass. The last of the orange sun could be seen through the trees in the orchard.

"I think you forgot the tonic," he said.

He stepped into the darkness also and searched for the light switch, but he could not find it. He kicked the leg of a chair. Then, swiftly and completely, he felt as if he was in his parents' house, walking *inside* through the darkness of his parents' house as a boy. He tried resisting the sensation but instead the years rushed away and left him eating a peanut butter sandwich in that distant kitchen, rain falling softly outside. In his ear, the ticking of that old familiar clock shaped in the face of a cat.

Then, standing trapped in the middle of darkness, the memory completely revealed itself. For this is what had happened, then, in the darkness: his foot had struck something. Not a chair. Something else. He looked down, the shape emerging out of shadows. The peanut butter sandwich tumbled through the air and fell soundlessly beside his mother's body. Her eyes closed and her face slightly greasy with makeup, she wore atop her head the little green hat he'd given her for Christmas. It was as if she had gotten dressed up and then died there on the floor, after arranging herself with arms crossed over her heart. Staggering, gasping, he backed away. He felt pain in the back of his head and realized he had backed into the wall trying to get away from the body, and then he lurched to his left and knocked a lamp off the table, which flashed blue as it crashed to the floor. Just then his mother's eyes opened. She turned her head to the side and smiled at him.

It's all right, Buddy, she said, sitting up. *It's all right. I was just pretending.*

A lamp lit the room.

"It's dark in here," Charlotte murmured, turning back to the window.

Clark pushed himself away from the wall. His eyes adjusted, the room reassembled, and he clearly saw now the figure of Charlotte sitting in a chair by the window in lamplight. His hairline was damp with sweat. Cautiously, he pressed his foot around on the carpet.

"You all right?" she said, not turning around.

He fell into a chair beside her. Mother is dead, he said to himself. Everyone who is dead is dead. And there's nobody here but us. The rest is a trick of the mind. He looked at Charlotte. The sun had gone all the way down by then. He could not image a single approach to the story.

PRETENDING

Clark sank into a chair in the back of the room and looked around. At the front of the room, Gordon Stanberry's face was illuminated by the overhead projector. Scrawled on the blackboard behind him were the words "Welcome Back to School."

Looking around, Clark found his colleagues vaguely unfamiliar. Who were these tanned, sexually satisfied looking people? During the school year, these same women were stiff and white-lipped, and Clark had often sat alone in the faculty room to avoid their tense, spittly, salad-flecked chatter. Now he could hardly recognize them. They lay against the children's desks with their large brown arms, sometimes casting backward looks at him, smiling and curious, as if they had just realized he was a man. He was having a difficult time listening to Stanberry, who was engaged in a very complicated recitation of rules and regulations for the impending school year, vast in its variation: Red day lunch at noon, Green day no gym, Orange day fire drill, Yellow day let's all take our pants off. Clark stared out the window.

Things were getting worse by the minute. The room was small and close, and his breath started coming faster, and he briefly indulged the conviction that Stanberry had barred the door. Red day yellow day ah ha ha ha ha. Only that morning, when Clark had to get out of bed for the in-service day, did he realize what a tremendous feat getting out of bed could be, a feat for the gods. He snapped to attention. Would anyone notice? Would anyone notice the bags under his eyes and the expression of pure panic? He felt possessed.

Several nights previous, his sense of disorientation in the house had become so strong that he called his sister, Mary, who under almost no circumstance was a sympathetic ear. He wanted to inquire very discreetly if she had been having trouble sleeping too, if she had been having some resultant questions about the properties of sleep versus waking, if she had felt not like Mary but like some uncooperative actor playing the part of Mary. Had she heard sneezing in her pantry? Contented burping down the hall? Did she feel like she was going a weensy bit nuts herself? But when he called, her belligerent husband, Jerome, had answered the phone by shouting *Yes? Yes?* and after quickly hanging up, Clark pictured an enormous hairy hand reaching into Jerome's bedroom window and dragging him out by the foot. How he had managed to hide all this from Charlotte was beyond him. He wanted to believe that she heard things in the house too. But if not, what? The blinking, uncomprehending stare. The loneliness of the truth. *You're crazy*.

"Clark?"

He raised his head. Standing over him was Mrs. Ormerod, the aged health teacher.

Clark looked around him.

"Are we done?" he said.

Mrs. Ormerod laughed. There wasn't anybody left in the room.

"God," said Clark, rubbing his eyes.

"Some daydream you must've been having," said Mrs. Ormerod. "Either that or a Stanberry-induced coma." The old lady leaned against Clark's desk, shaking her head. "Listen. Let's go. Why don't you give Mrs. O a ride? I'm out your way."

Clark looked up at Mrs. Ormerod's cap of white hair. He liked Mrs. Ormerod. She had a truncated plastic torso she carried under her arm during the school year, with little red ovaries and a real anal opening through which she occasionally thrust, for some pedagogical reason or another, bottle cleaners. She had been one of the few teachers who was nice to him the previous winter when he'd taken over for the ailing Mr. St. Paul. Clark nodded, and they walked through the empty halls into the bright late-summer sunlight.

They drove together past the small houses of Clementine, past the corner stores with kids holding orange and purple freeze-pops and staring as they passed, winding their way up out of the small concavity in which the town was built. People sat clustered in the shade of small trees, reaching into coolers, talking softly. Each street was like a sovereign nation, and people looked normal and cheerful separately, but when you put it all together, the town didn't quite make sense to Clark. Two children on bicycles darted out across the street.

"You like our little town so far?" asked Mrs. Ormerod.

"Sure," said Clark, braking hard. He nodded his head. He thought hard about what to say.

"It's rough to be the new people. Hard to break in."

"True," said Clark. "That's true." Clark looked out the window, then glanced over at Mrs. Ormerod. "Hey," he said. "Mrs. Health Teacher. I've got a question for you."

"Shoot," said the old lady. "Is it about sex?"

"Not really," said Clark. "Is there any sort of illness that has—" he smirked as if to discredit his own question, "hallucination as a symptom?"

"Sure," said Mrs. Ormerod. "Senility, for example."

"No, no," said Clark. "For somebody my age. What if somebody, say, my age, is confused a lot. He isn't sleeping well, so he mopes around all day. You know. Sometimes he's so tired he can hardly even listen to what anybody's saying. And his mind is lazy and kind of apathetic and follows any crazy thought that comes along. I mean some really crazy thoughts . . ."

"Well," said Mrs. Ormerod. "Is there particular hardship in his life? Particular events? Stress?"

"No. Not anymore, that is. Why?"

"Well, maybe he's just sad."

"Sad?" laughed Clark. "*Sad*?"

"Stressed-out. Pushed. And probably pretty tired from, you know, not sleeping. Sleeplessness can induce hallucination." Mrs. Ormerod laughed back uncertainly. She withdrew a Kleenex from her sleeve and wiped it across her brow.

Clark stared hard at the road. He felt that he had finally said too much, and he resented Mrs. Ormerod. Now she thought she understood. She didn't understand whatsoever. There were *things* in that house. Or else he was losing his mind. And yet, in saying so, he was isolated and reduced and merely "sad." He remembered similar looks, similar pitying glances from people in the past, speaking to him of his mother.

Suddenly Mrs. Ormerod leaned forward and peered through her glasses.

"Will you look at that," she said, pointing.

They were coming up quickly behind a small, motorized vehicle on the shoulder, going at a dangerously slow speed. The rider of the vehicle turned around and blinked against the wind, pasting her hair back with one hand.

"Oh my God," said Clark.

"Sure is a strange thing to do," said Mrs. Ormerod. "Ride a tractor in a nice dress. Now why would a person do a strange thing like that?"

Clark rubbed his hand hard against his brow.

"You know that lady?"

"Yes," said Clark. "That's my wife."

"That's your wife? On that little tractor?"

"It's a lawn mower," said Clark.

Mrs. Ormerod opened her mouth. Then she stuck her head out the window and brought it back in, just as they blew past.

"What in heaven's name is she doing on the road with a *lawn* mower?" marveled Mrs. Ormerod, looking back.

Clark didn't say anything.

"Well for Pete's sakes stop," cried the old lady. "Back up. Let's ask her."

Clark brought the car to a stop, then rolled backward until pulling even with the tractor mower. Charlotte sat straight and primly upon it with both hands on the wheel and her purse hanging from her shoulder. Clark rolled down his window.

"Charlotte?" he said.

She looked over at him. It was Charlotte, all right.

"Hello, Clark," she said, rolling past.

Clark pulled forward. "Hello," he said. "What are you doing?"

"Hello, Charlotte!" shouted Mrs. Ormerod from the passenger seat. "It's so nice to finally meet you. I've heard so much about you. We love having your husband at our school!"

Charlotte nodded and waved. They were moving slowly alongside each other, the mower chugging along the shoulder. Oncoming cars flew past with open, staring faces in them.

"What are you doing on that tractor?" called Mrs. Ormerod.

"It's a sit-down mower," said Charlotte. "A Power C-465 with an adjustable rotor."

"Well, it's very nice."

"Clark got it at the Agway. It was very expensive. We never use it, so . . ."

"So . . ." said Clark.

"So I decided to get out and take it for a spin. It's kind of like a second car, really."

"OK, get off," said Clark. "Pull over and get off right now."

"No," said Charlotte. "I'm doing something."

"What the hell are you doing?"

"I'm having fun," said Charlotte archly.

"You know what?" shouted Mrs. Ormerod over the wind, "I ought to go get myself one of those!"

The two women shared a laugh.

Clark steadied his voice. "Cut it out," he said. "You are not crazy."

"Oh yeah?" Charlotte leaned over close enough to put her hand on the window. Her seed pearl necklace jostled against her neck and her chin trembled. "I've got my problems too, Clark. I've got things that need attention too. You don't even *no*tice anymore."

"Watch out," shouted Clark.

Charlotte jerked the mower to the right, just missing the pothole. She looked back. "Jeez," she said. "This thing handles nicely."

"People," Clark rasped. "People will see you."

"People!" cried Charlotte, her purse strap falling down around her wrist. "I don't know people. I don't know anybody. Nobody talks to me. This town is creepy! Nobody talks to me or says hello or asks me how I am. Not once! I live on a deserted *island*, Clark. With you."

"What the hell's that supposed to mean?"

"Are you all right, dear?" asked Mrs. Ormerod, reaching out her hand.

"She's not crazy," said Clark numbly. "She's just pretending."

"That's right," said Charlotte. "I *never* get to be the crazy one."

"Who on earth would want to be crazy?" crowed Mrs. Ormerod.

"Don't knock it 'til you try it," said Charlotte.

Behind them, several cars had gathered and were trailing at a snail's pace. The driver in the front car leaned on his horn.

"Fine," Clark said in a low voice, setting his jaw. "All right. You want me to just drive away and leave you? Is that what you want? Since you're so completely alone?"

Charlotte looked off at the passing trees. She smoothed down the fluttering collar of her dress.

"No," she said quietly. "At the present moment, I'm lost."

They drove on next to each other for another moment. Nobody said anything. They began to climb a hill.

"Hey. Lean forward a little," suggested Clark.

In his rearview mirror, he could see a growing line of cars going up the hill behind them, windshields glinting. The man behind them tried to pass, and was forced back into line by an oncoming truck.

"Up here," said Clark, pointing. "Up here you can take a right. Go all the way up and take another right. Do you know your way home from that little farm? Near to the TV tower?"

"Yes," said Charlotte. "All right. Yes. I think so."

"All right," said Clark, looking out at her warily.

"All right," said Charlotte.

They drove along side by side for another moment.

"So I'll see you at home?" said Clark.

"Yes," said Charlotte. "I'll see you."

"So nice to meet you!" cried Mrs. Ormerod.

"You too," said Charlotte.

He could see her in his rear view mirror, rising up over the crest of the hill, gripping the small wheel. The way she looked, going so slowly, it was like a mirage. A distortion. Like somebody rising up out of heat.

THE NEXT LIFE

The seniors did not swim in the water so much as wrestle with it. They slapped at the surface with long, ropy arms. They swam with their heads buried in the water, legs trailing behind in a dead way, and when they swam the backstroke, they reached behind themselves tentatively, as if walking backward down a long staircase. Sometimes a bathing cap would sink under the surface altogether, only to reappear after a long moment, followed by a hardened paunch or a set of breasts cresting out like a chain of islands. Watching them from the poolside grass, Clark decided that in the next life, he wanted to be born with gills. Underwater, as in dreams, a body has no weight and no consequence. In the next life, he didn't want to be bound to dirt and houses and names and other things that sink.

These days, these very last days of summer, Clark slept for one or two hours before sunrise, at which point he would rise and dress for the pool. He liked the house in the early morning. It was very quiet then. No coughing. No crying. The voices, the spirits—whatever they were—were late to get up, almost as if they were just regular, lazy people. They left him alone in the morning.

He'd leave the house before Charlotte awoke. He had become ashamed of himself, but shame was not a teaching feeling, nor was it sociable. When he left Charlotte asleep, pressed to her side of the bed, hair trailing behind her on the pillow, she sometimes smiled in her dreams, and it made him glad to see her smile, and he also knew she was smiling in a reality untroubled by his presence.

That morning, towel over his shoulder, he'd walked through the yard, past the lawn mower with its For Sale sign hung askew from the handle, and down the middle of the road to the busy street at the foot of the hill. He could hear his bare feet slap across the macadam. It had not yet rained, and the ends of the leaves were beginning to curl up and yellow.

He arrived to the pool just as the seniors paraded in, in full dress, the men wearing seersucker pants and blue shirts thin and flat as rice paper. The women's hair, permed into fine gray aureoles, was rather like clusters of heliotrope. It really got to Clark, how they were dressed up to go to the pool. Clark himself had come shirtless, which now struck him as obscene. In an hour and a half, it would no longer be Senior Swim but Public Swim, and the whole raucous town, people like him who had their whole lives left to swim, their whole lives to take their shirts off, would come and steal this little peace.

The seniors did not speak much to each other, and they were not friendly to him. This made sense. Why should dying people be friendly, when they can finally be however they please?

He had not come to bother anybody. He sat on the grass, looking down at his feet. He watched the pool water through his toes. Late the previous night, his four millionth sleepless night that summer, it occurred to him that he had never thought about death. He never thought about what death was really like. As a child, death is introduced to a person in black, ragged cloaks—a kind of villain. Then, some night, some sleepless night in that person's twenty-ninth year, watching the moon rise in the sky like some fabulous prize, it occurs to him that death is just the other thing that can happen. One of two indifferent options. He had acquired a new appreciation for the morbidity of philosophers and artists. He had acquired an appreciation for the attractiveness of death to crazy people. He looked up at the sky. It seemed very close. Where did the sky begin if not right above your head? All the dead walking on top of your head and shoulders, murmuring and conferring and coughing. His own mother walking up and down his back, mutely shouting her instructions, as the audience in the cineplex cautions the hero. He moved his stiff neck under the weight.

A child walked onto the pool grounds, carrying a pink towel tied with a string. He hesitated at the mouth of the gate, talking to himself, scouting the grassy ridge. Once he fixed on a spot, he walked along the deck with his eyes on it. He did not walk so much like a boy, but more gravely, like someone who spends a great deal of time gazing at equations. Under his thick glasses, his eyes appeared large and rabbit-like, and his hair still showed the tines of a comb. It was the little boy from the volleyball court. Judy's brother—James Nye.

Clark raised his hand, but the boy did not see. A tetherball swung from a pole behind the swimming pool. James Nye lay his towel down on the grass and began to hit the tetherball to himself. Mostly, his fist only grazed the ball, which caused it to ricochet into his face and knock off his glasses. The few times he actually made contact with the ball, it came around and hit him in the back of the head. He proceeded to stalk himself in this manner for some time. Satisfied, he went to the far corner of the deep end and stuck his legs in the pool.

Clark cheered up watching the kid tool around, his counterpart on the other side of the pool, only a shiny film screen in between replaying on a loop the movie of the sky. To be a boy again, he thought, smiling, to live in a world of small challenges.

The boy unfolded his towel and withdrew a deflated set of yellow water wings. He put his mouth up to the air valve and began to blow, but was simultaneously squeezing the air back out with his grip. He caught Clark's interested gaze in the process, and returned an averted smile.

Suddenly, the boy stood up and looked out toward the shallow end. An old woman in a skirted bathing suit was jumping up and down, shouting hoarsely.

"What is it?" Clark said aloud.

The lifeguard shot up in his chair and leapt out over the water. Up in the sky, the kid kicked his spindly legs. His red windbreaker bellowed up with air. Clark watched with dispassion, finding himself too tired even for tragedy. The boy came crashing down into the water. The old woman clung to his chest.

"There's a snake," she sobbed, "a snake in the pool."

Then, coming down the lap lanes in successive shouts, like the calling down a coal shaft:

A snake in the pool!
A snake in the pool!
There's a snake in the pool!

The swimmers turned to one another, their cheeks suddenly in high color. Then they looked down below their treading feet, where they could see and yet not see, through the refracted surface, the poisonous man-eating North American chlorinated water snake. Then they began to paddle frantically to the ladders. Several had already started to climb out, but they climbed with such great slowness. Their elephantine feet groped for the rungs. Those who were left in the water gathered in human clots around each ladder, crying out, *Hurry! Hurry! Do you want us to be bitten by the snake?* In the middle of the shallow end, in the middle of the snake pit, Gundars stood slobbering, searching the water.

Clark rose and went to the ladders, dusting off his hands. He held his hand out to the swimmers left treading in the deep end, but they refused it. "We need the *ladder*," one woman snapped. So instead, he knelt by the edge and waited for one of them to talk to him, but they didn't.

By the time the last of them were clearing the ladders, the lifeguard emerged clutching a short, black length of hose.

"It's merely a hosse!" he announced, his voice breaking. "Merely a hosse having fallen into!"

A hose!

A hose?

He says it's only a piece of hose that fell in!

The seniors turned to one another again, water dripping in rivers off their hard bellies. They pat one another on the back and hand. Their hairdos were ruined, and their faces, exhilarated. A hose! Clark knelt there, watching them.

Whadid he say?

A hose.

A hose, not a snake!

It was then that Clark noticed the water wings. They were sitting poolside, limp, softly deflating. Clark stood. A glare covered the pool, throwing back the dim sky and its fringe of trees. He walked toward the deep end and looked down into the blue. And when the water began to calm, he could see that there was something large in the pool. Under the surface, and sinking. The outline became clear, as an obvious idea at long last reveals itself to the mind, and Clark felt that a smarter man might've already prevented it.

"James," he said.

He was suddenly aware of great distances, of the distance between him and everyone else, between the deep end and the shallow end, which seemed very, very, far away, in another country. He recognized, on some level, that the teenage lifeguard would have to swim across the pool into the deep end, whereas he would only have to jump. Besides, in all the agitation, the kid was still rejoicing, the length of hose held over his head like a flaccid rifle. And the seniors were rejoicing. They suddenly seemed very, very young and absurdly unsuspecting, like characters in a children's book.

Then Clark experienced a moment of pointed clarity. A moment of doubtlessness. A kind of unbearable knowledge, unbearably right—heretofore hidden this whole, dreadful summer, his whole life perhaps—cut through the fog in his mind. What was real? Well, *this* was real. He and the pool and the boy were the realest things on earth at the moment. He heard the water's gentle nickering in the gutters, soft laughter from inside. And then he heard his own mortal heart call in response.

Kagung. Kagung. Kagung.

It was a lonely moment. But as he felt himself dive into the water, its coolness encompassing him and burying him inside, he recognized it as one of the more sensual moments in his life. He felt the voluptuousness of being born for a reason, of being valuable. He spun around and around under water, his skin covered in bubbles.

He opened his eyes. For a moment, with his body arrested at the end of its dive, he could not tell which direction was up. He was in a box of water. All four walls were the same color. Then, looking over his shoulder, he saw the boy several feet below, or beside, hovering upright, kicking faintly. James Nye pushed at the water with his elbows, as if he were jockeying with other boys and not with his own end. His dark hair was softly wavering. And although his face was white and his mouth contorted, his gaze rested upon nothing but a pair of eyeglasses that lay below him, in the far semi-darkness. How odd it was to be standing above the boy in such a silent room, no words passing between them, gazing at such a relic of life as a pair of eyeglasses.

Feeling himself drawing away from the boy, Clark fought the tightness and the coldness until he had a hold of the boy's slippery arm, and there they were, in a sort of friendly confrontation, at the bottom of the pool.

James looked up at him, hovering there, his eyes the same color as the pool. His mouth was open and the tongue was lolling in and out. Still the boy looked pleased, as one is pleased to see a friend in a dream.

Then, just before his eyes began to roll back, the boy raised his arms, and this gesture seemed utterly familiar to Clark. It was a gesture that anyone who was ever a child made a hundred times if he made it once, and it meant *Carry me*.

Yes, thought Clark. *I'll carry you.*

PART TWO

EMERGENCY

The automated doors of the supermarket opened, and Charlotte stepped into the refrigerated air. Through the plate-glass window, the day outside looked somehow painted or contained, the trees bowing in their late summer heaviness. Humming, she walked through the pyramids of oranges and peppers and melons, and then brought her hand basket to one of the registers. The woman in front of her, wearing culottes and a somewhat dyspeptic expression, paid for her groceries and pushed them out the doors. She moved slowly out across the macadam parking lot, her cart glinting in the sun.

Just then, an ambulance streaked into view. The checkout girl at Charlotte's register stopped and put her hands over her ears and shut her eyes. The despondent sound of the siren filled the building, coming and going. When it was over, the checkout girl lowered her hands. She turned and looked outside.

"Poor somebody," she said. She was a young girl, wearing thick blue eye shadow, her eyes round as pennies. "On a beautiful summer day like this. Accidents shouldn't be allowed."

"God shouldn't allow them," agreed the heavyset check-out girl at the register next to them. Both girls resumed moving the items mechanically over the sensors. Charlotte's girl scraped a carton of eggs over the sensor several times, then looked at it irritably.

"A shame," she said, looking straight at Charlotte, "on a day like this."

"Oh," said Charlotte. "You mean the ambulance? It probably wouldn't be nice to be in an ambulance on any sort of day."

The girl nodded appreciatively. "True," she said. "Would you rather die on a pretty day or a rainy day, Marly?"

"Rainy," responded the chubby girl without looking.

"I hate sirens," said the checkout girl, "I hate sirens and dogs barking. And screaming. Ugly sounds. I hate ugly sounds."

"Well," said Charlotte. "It's part of life, I guess."

"What is?"

"Death," Charlotte shrugged. "Sure, death. Ugly sounds and ugly things. Accidents." She smiled at the girl.

"You wouldn't say that if that was you," the girl replied, gesturing with her thumb out the window.

"Yes I would," said Charlotte. "I would after a while."

"I guess," said the girl. "Yeah, I guess so. After being dead a while I guess you just have to accept it."

"Ghosts don't," said Marly.

"No, they don't," agreed the checkout girl.

"My uncle, he lives in a stigmatized property. Do you know what that means?"

Charlotte and the checkout girl shook their heads.

"A crime of passion happened there and a lady shot her

husband. My uncle got a good deal on it. Because nobody wants to live in a bad luck place. You can buy up those stigmatized properties if you're smart."

"What a load of junk," snorted the checkout girl. "If you've got something coming to you, you got it coming."

Charlotte looked outside again at the blank, sunny day. She felt suddenly suspicious of it. She didn't want to go outside. She wanted to stay in the grocery store, talking with these two girls, as if she herself was still young and underemployed and unaccountable for the things she said.

"Seventeen dollars and five cents," said the checkout girl, holding out her hand.

"Wait, wait," said Charlotte. With an awkward laugh, she took a chocolate bar from the rack and laid it on the belt. The girl put her foot on a pedal and the chocolate bar moved along toward her.

"Doesn't that make your teeth hurt?" the girl asked.

"I love chocolate," Charlotte confided.

"I do too," said Marly.

"I eat it in secret," said Charlotte.

"Me too," said Marly. "Alone."

"Oh God," the first checkout girl said, her shoulders tensing. "Here comes another one."

This time, the sound of the siren rose up as if from the ground. When the ambulance passed, the whole building trembled again with the sound. All the customers stood still, faces slack, listening. The two-ness of the ambulances had caught their attention. The vehicle edged through the intersection, screaming, then raced on.

The girl relaxed her shoulders. She sighed and handed Charlotte her bag of groceries.

"Two ambulances," said the girl. "That's not a good sign. That's not a good sign at all. A big accident or something. A double murder."

"A double murder on a Monday morning?" scoffed Marly.

The young girl looked back outside where there wasn't anything left but some traffic and traffic lights changing. "I guess I'd rather die on a pretty day," the girl said to no one. "When there was quiet. If I had a choice."

"Well, you don't get a choice," said Marly. "Zip zap, it's over. Nobody comes around with a menu."

"How do you know," said the girl earnestly. "You don't."

Charlotte lifted her bag off the belt. There was something then, something that made her shiver. The cold supermarket air? She crossed to the automated doors, and they opened for her. Behind her, the checkout girls were peering into their sensors, trying to divine what they said.

LIFE LIKE BREAD

An hour later, Charlotte was racing down a very slick hospital hallway, clutching her purse to her stomach. When she slipped turning a corner, the purse fell to the floor spilling pennies. The purse behind her, she ran now with her hands out like a blind woman. The faces of the orderlies congregating by the candy machines were indifferent to her, their kingdom of halls stretching out with cold brightness, and somewhere in this labyrinth, Clark passed her going the other direction on a gurney. His face was pale and bloated and full of tubes, his not-quite-shut eyes now horrifying in their loveliness, and Charlotte almost let him pass by, right out of the realm of nightmare, before pursuing. And even then she only clutched the pillow where his head was, unable even to speak his name and hence identify herself as his wife. The speed of the gurney pulled her along, the breathing of the orderly loud in her ear. Soon her hand was removed from his pillow, and the gurney disappeared between two swinging doors, and she stood there, absolutely still—tearless, nonexistent—until someone lead her to a chair.

The boy Clark had tried to save in the swimming pool was taken to a separate hospital for children. She was glad he was not there, because the first time they wheeled Clark out of the ER that afternoon, his innocent and cold-looking feet sticking off the end of the gurney, Charlotte found herself full of unimaginable violence. She hated that boy. She was furious, and her fists trembled with nothing in them, and she was angry at this strange town, which had lured them there, and for what? For dead-end jobs and for fighting and for sinking and for losing?

Amidst the impersonal sounds of machinery and the squeaking of doctors' shoes in the hallway running somewhere else, Charlotte waited at his bedside. By then, her anger had abandoned her. For she saw that life was merely proving what she already suspected of it—its essential infidelity. Its caprice. For once you're born, she knew, the world that brought you forth so arrogantly washes its hands of you. It recuses itself. She knew all this long ago.

When the doctors came to Charlotte, she tried to concentrate very hard on the things they were saying but somehow she had already managed to imprison herself into widowhood. He looked so *dead*. You could say he was sleeping a thousand times and he still looked dead. And if he was dead, how was it there remained so much left to tell him? Looking at his handsome, long-jawed face, the doctors rattling on, at last tears stung her eyes. For there was so much left to tell him. She wanted to tell him it was all right, that he wasn't a freak. She was. She was the freak! She was the one so afraid of losing things, so freakishly afraid, that he was the first person she had ever dared love since the day she was taken screaming from her mother, for surely she had screamed then, those many years ago. And now, she could barely say I love you without blushing, as if it were a perversion. She inched along through life, a woman on a crossbeam. She wanted to tell him that perhaps if it had been different, if she had lived in a different world, a brighter childhood, she might have been capable of dreaming of the things he dreamed of. What? A child of their own, opening a book of fairytales on the carpet? She leaned closer, trying to see into those half-closed eyes.

"Clark," she said. "Love."

She stayed hovering like that, crouching almost, waiting for his eyes to open, until one of the doctors made her take a pill in a white cup and she felt her mind cloud over as she fell asleep in a chair, beside that body a thousand nights familiar.

Morning broke. She was awoken by a tap on the head and found herself staring into the eyes of her husband. Of all things, he was grinning, his long, brown arms stretching out from his white paper dress. His jowls were swollen as if they were still engorged with water. For a moment, before she was fully awake, she thought the squeaking wheels of gurneys were birdsong, and that she and Clark were back at home. And perhaps they were. He laughed. She laughed too. She didn't want to laugh. She wanted to be angry. She climbed onto the gurney, kissing his face.

"You're alive!" she cried. "You jackass!"

She embraced him with her whole body. He looked astonished, his blue eyes wide open, taking in every inch of the room. And then the nurses marched in with their cold-headed instruments and their angry flirting. The doctors came and conferred with Charlotte and she once again hardly heard anything they said. A reporter from the *Daily Clementine* materialized with his camera, the flash filled the room, and she saw Clark pose gamely from his bed, hands folded in front of him.

Late that evening, they let him go. When they walked down the hall, Clark in hospital slippers and a borrowed exercise suit, everyone clapped. The news of his heroic actions had spread through the wards, and all those who were healing or dying in their beds, sutured or medicated, suffering from ailments with no poetry in them, took heart.

Nobody, including Clark, knew exactly why it had taken three minutes to rescue James Nye from the water. Gundars had fainted, and all the old folks could do was gather around the deep end and shout and stomp their feet. Drowning victims sometimes panic, dragging down their saviors, but Clark did not remember a struggle. He could not remember anything after diving in, seeing the kid, the kid reaching up, and experiencing a feeling of supreme patience and assuredness, the ridiculousness of making appointments.

Three treacherous minutes later, he'd reached the surface and lost consciousness. The seniors dragged him to the deck as he began to sink back down. A veteran of the Korean War gave him CPR, after helping the kid first. The child was not breathing. They were both unconscious to the world.

Where was he, those hours? Clark did not try to describe his half-death, and Charlotte did not ask. She only wanted to be quiet and walk quietly, so as not to disturb the Fates and have them reverse their decision. She turned on all the lights in the house and made a bed for him on the sofa where she could be near at all times. In the kitchen, opening a can of peaches for him, her hands shook so wildly that she had to tell him there were no peaches. News reached them later that same day that James Nye was alive and there was no apparent brain damage. This news made Clark take a deep breath, raise his fist to his mouth, and begin to cry.

"Don't cry!" Charlotte said, wringing her hands. "Please don't cry!"

The doctors had told her that he shouldn't be upset or exerted for several days. But there was nothing she could do. Putting her hands over the leaks did not stop them. The amount of tears was copious. His smooth olive face was wet with them. So she sat and watched. It occurred to her she had never seen him cry this freely, not even upon burying his mother.

For several days afterward, Clark convalesced at home, reveling in the rather morbid attentions of strangers without resenting them for never coming around beforehand. The Ribbendrops came bearing a vat of soup, friendlier and less bloodless than they had appeared through their car window. Beautiful Meg Girgis came and sat at the kitchen table, holding Charlotte's hand, shaking her glossy head. Vice-Principal Stanberry, a yahoo nevertheless, showed up with flowers. Even the mayor of Clementine called and recited a poem about courage over the telephone.

Charlotte was half-ingested by the mailbox, fishing out all the letters and newspaper clippings, when she heard Clark calling from inside the yellow house, "Charlotte! Charlotte!"

She slogged back up to the door through the rain.

"Hold on!" she cried back, "Hold on, sweetheart! I'm coming!"

She ran into the living room, only to find him safe on the sofa under his checkered blanket, looking rapturously out the window at the hawthorn tree.

"It's got flowers," he said, pointing. His eyes were wide and limpid, and the top of his shirt was misbuttoned.

"Jesus," said Charlotte, hand on her heart. She dropped her umbrella to the floor. "Sweetheart, it's had flowers for weeks. God, I thought something was the matter." She exhaled and sat beside him and began to fix his buttons.

Clark smiled serenely, lifting his chin. Something *was* the matter, he realized—he had not seen those beautiful flowers for weeks. Surely, seeing the flowers now was a sign that he was back, he was literally back to his senses. His old self. He had not been able to see the flowers before because he was not really there. Yes, he'd been under a curse—a ridiculous curse of sadness and delusion and wallowing in memory. In the past several days of bed rest alone, he had seen a hundred things that assured him he was cured: a family of goldfinches was making its nest in the eaves, a hole in the hedges announced a hedgehog in the mornings, and the important shapes of birds and airplanes slid across the yard, all seen to his eyes. This was *it*, he said to himself. Life—faithful, manifest, like bread. No fake things, no tricks or illusions. He craned his neck upward as Charlotte fixed his shirt. No mysterious footsteps moved overhead. No one sneezed in the pantry. The house felt normal and fine and sunny.

And his wife. His wife was his wife. He nearly laughed aloud with the pleasure of this. He could hardly believe the beautiful lunacy of such a pretty girl sticking by him simply because he asked her to! Whenever he said her name, there she appeared through a doorway. Marriage! Why does one do it? Clark decided right then that marriage wasn't outrageous at all. It was simple and it was brilliant. It was the building of an army—love's four-handed army.

He took Charlotte's hand and pulled her close to him.

"What?" she said.

"Shut up," he said. He touched her face. He took a fistful of her wet blonde hair and turned it around on his fist. It was like gathering honey on a wooden spool. He promised himself that, as long as he could reason, he would not take her for granted again. Not her, not the blossoms, not the soft light that crept under the bedroom door in the morning. A gift, he thought, his eyes moistening, she was his daily-given gift. *Wife.*

"Hello," he said, sticking out his hand. "My name is Clark."

"I know that," she said.

"My name is Clark," he said. "What's your name?"

"Charlotte."

"A pleasure to meet you, Charlotte."

Charlotte looked at him.

"You want me to shake your hand?" she said.

"I want you to shake my hand," he said. "Let's pretend like we just met."

Her eyes fluttered. She didn't move. And then, he almost said it—*I'm sorry*—because he was, he was sorry. But the words caught in his throat, falling short.

"Hey listen," he said, neatening her hair. "You were right about me. I've been somewhere else. Who knows where?

Preoccupied. Kind of strange. But I'm back now. All right? I'm back now to my old self. I swear it. Let's start fresh."

As for Charlotte, she stared back at him, searching his face for a sign of derision or untrustworthiness. But she could not find one. His gaze was warm, heavy with love. She straightened where she sat. Some beautiful fluttering hopeful thing inside her chest hopped from rib to rib. And for a second, the world seemed revolutionizable, a place in which it was possible to transcend one's fearfulness or motherlessness or one's long-cherished bitterness toward the Fates. The roads and the desk jobs and the chores and the zippers and hospitals fell away with that look, and there she was for a single moment—Charlotte Eugenia Adair— nothing between her and her great promise. She trembled. Yes, yes, she thought. I am she.

"Shall I . . ." said Charlotte. "I'll get you something to eat. The usual? A mayonnaise sandwich?"

"God no," said Clark, laughing as perhaps a man laughs when he realizes he is dead and safe in heaven. "All that's over. No more crazy stuff. I swear to you right now, Charlotte. I'll never eat mayonnaise again in my entire life."

Charlotte covered her mouth and laughed too. Outside, there was a clap of retreating thunder. Clark seized the umbrella and opened it over their heads, spraying them with water. Charlotte lay down beside him.

"Thank God it's raining finally," she said. "I like the rain."

"Hey," said Clark. "Play the harmonica for me."

"What? I don't own a harmonica."

"Dance around in a circle for me."

"What?" Charlotte squealed. "No!"

"Roll around on the ground for me. Bounce up and down for me."

"No!"

"Then sing the song about the duck with the yellow shoes," he murmured. "I'm convalescing. You're supposed to do what I *say*."

Charlotte swallowed, took a breath. The song was one of the happy things she remembered from being a kid. When it rained, you sang it. "Ooh, wasn't it a *bit* of luck that *I* was born a baby duck. With yellow socks—"

"—and yellow shoes—"

"So *I* may go wherever I choose. Quack quack quack . . ."

And after they sang for a bit, they were silent. They lay together under the shared blue shade of the umbrella, watching a finch drink from the baby pool outside, which was now filled so generously with rainwater.

GRATITUDE

"I can see your epiglottis," he said, leaning over her.

This sent Charlotte into fits of laughter all over again.

"Look look," he said, pointing. "Now it's boinging up and down."

"Stop!" she cried, drying her eyes, sitting upright in her pink nightgown. "Stop. That's enough. I should get up and do something."

"You are doing something," he said. "You're my nursie."

"No," she said. "I mean clean or organize things or something. I can't stay home from work forever, you know. I can't take care of you forever. We'll both be fired. What will we live on?"

"Love," Clark said. "Love and air."

"Come on," she said, looking away. "You're all better and I know it. We can't play hooky forever."

"I can play hooky a little longer," he said. "I don't want to go back to that gym-socky school. Besides, it's raining. I can't go out in the rain. Let's build an ark."

"What about those poor kids? What'll they do without your guidance?"

"They'd be a hell of a lot better off going it blind," said Clark. "Let's go to the movies."

"The movies? It's nine a.m. on a Thursday."

"Hey Charlotte," he said, pressing his nose up with his fingers to make a pig face, "It's never too late to have a happy childhood!"

She laughed and pushed him away. "Oh yes it is."

He leapt on top of her and grabbed her wrists. "I feel great. I feel like new. I feel like I just goddamned met you." Then he sat back on his haunches. "Hey. I've got an idea."

He stood beside the bed, naked but for his socks. Slowly, he pulled the blanket off the bed. He turned and looked back at her with that look.

"No way," Charlotte said, looking at the blanket. "Not that."

"Yes," he said.

"No!" she cried, laughing. "Please not that!"

"Yes," he repeated, almost gently. He put the blanket over his head and stood up, draped in it. His hands went out in the shape of claws. "I am Swamp Monster, and you're my prey."

"No I am not!" she cried. He loomed over her. She tried to reason with him. "Wait! I have to go to the bathroom first!"

"Too late!" the Swamp Monster roared, as she screamed and shot out of bed. She stood panting on the other side. "Swamp Monster *hungry*," he said. One large claw swiped out at her.

"Hey!" she said. "Can you see through the holes?"

He scuttled around the bed.

"But I *hate* being chased and I *hate* being tickled," she said. "You know that."

The monster dropped his stiff arms. "Do you want to be It, then?" he asked.

Charlotte shifted her weight, trying to gain a preemptive advantage. Then, screaming, she clambered over the bed and began to run. Behind her, he pursued, making his low hungry sounds, trotting after her stiff-legged, stiff-armed, tapping the walls with his hands. The floors shook. She screamed with laughter. He wondered briefly, what if the neighbors saw them through the windows? He smiled under his blanket. He was cheating. He could see her through the holes. Her hair fluttered behind her like ribbons against her nightshirt. Inside the next doorway, he saw her turn and wait, biting her hand. She was trapped. He felt an actual monster hunger for her. Breathing rapaciously, he closed in.

Then his head smacked the top of the doorjamb. "Ow," he said. He was momentarily blind with pain. She screamed and escaped around him down the hall.

"Swamp Monster angry now," he said.

"It's not my fault!" Charlotte sang, running to the top of the stairwell. "It's not my fault you hit your head!"

She skated around the banister, her face bright and child-like with the chase. Perhaps he was right. Perhaps it was not too late. He was loping down the hall toward her at great speed. She looked down the staircase. Inspired, she ran down the stairs.

"Hmmm," the Swamp Monster said. Above her, on the landing, he sniffed the air. "I smell *woman!*"

One socked foot sensed the air, tapped the first tread. Blanketed, grunting, he stepped heavily down the stair.

"No fair!" Charlotte screamed. "You *can* see through the holes!"

But still she waited for him at the bottom, wild with the gratitude that is love. The blanket snagged somewhere on the tread and began to rise up the monster's naked front, exposing the dark, hairy groin.

"*Clark*," Charlotte said.

"Who Clark?" grunted the Swamp Monster sincerely.

Stair by stair he descended, until his draped form was upon her.

"No." she said. "No. *Please* don't tickle me. Have mercy!"

"Swamp Monster in love," he said from under his blanket. "Tickle the way he show love."

He seized her. She began to shriek. This half-ecstatic, horrified protestation could be heard even in the street, where it was raining.

TRUE STORIES

On his first day alone in the house, the sky cleared. The trees were left rain-glossy and intensely green. Clark pressed his face against the living room window. Charlotte had returned to her duties at Ziff Negligence, and the house seemed particularly empty. He put on his mud shoes and gray sweatpants. The world outside, as green and alive as he felt himself, was calling for him.

He stepped out into the gusty air. This was the sort of wind that blew only at the far end of summertime, a hot wind, an ushering-out. He remembered that in the hospital and through a drugged haze he had watched a television program about weather. The program was one of the first things he saw after waking from his drowned sleep, and he remembered it vividly. He also remembered the self-possessed voice of the narrator in his ears. In the moments before he realized where he was, he thought the voice was God's.

He crossed the road to the orchard, whistling. Field birds were singing, and the low, steamy clouds hurried out to sea. The grass was beaten down and sun-bleached, and he found himself peeling sticks off trees and then whipping them into the tall grasses, scaring up the funny crickets that hopped up funnily as if sprung.

He lay down, right then and there, in the wet grass. The sky was a pearly gray, and the wind carried the smell of hot soil and overripe apples and the end of summer. He smiled to himself. He was back! He was back, but better. His head was clear. He didn't feel hot or thick or used up or dogged by strange preoccupations. The wet September wind blew through his skin as if it were mere cheesecloth.

Day by day, throughout his convalescence, he had secretly been coming up with a Plan. He had never had a Plan. But now he wanted one. He wanted to change his life around. He was going to quit his job at the school, just as soon as he could manage to get back into his collared shirt and show up. He never liked it and he wasn't any good at saying the things he was supposed to, not to mention all those skipped night classes. What he really wanted was to work for a newspaper. He wanted to write frank, true stories about normal people out of luck. He wanted one of those Remingtons like his father's and he wanted to hear the click tap ching of his thoughts being iterated. He wanted Charlotte leaning over his shoulder, laughing at what he wrote, holding a glass of wine. And in the distance behind her, perhaps, a small child carrying a doll for Daddy?

He rolled on his side and stared hard at the small yellow house in the distance, half-hidden by the trunks of the apple trees. He screwed his eyes. There was still something wrong about it. It was a nice house, but maybe it wasn't their house. All those sounds and shadows, that abandoned music, perhaps he had not made it up. Maybe he hadn't made it up at all, maybe the *house* was crazy. It was almost as if the house was heartbroken and thinking of somebody else. Sometimes he thought of Bob and Marion Lippet running to their car, screeching away without a word. Why? And were they happier now?

He would march right home and say it. He'd say, Let's sell the place. I know, it's ridiculous. But let's sell. Let's just drive away now, while the going's good.

He stood, squaring his shoulders. An apple fell with a thud to the orchard floor. He picked it up and shined it on his shirt. His teeth broke the skin easily, sweet sourness filling his mouth. Later, he would do it. The house would still be there when he came back from his walk. He would say it later.

DUMBWAITER

The car ground to a stop in the driveway and Charlotte looked through the windshield at the house, rooms lighted in the early evening. Smiling, she removed the pins from her hair. She knew that when she walked in he would be engaged in one of his Pyrrhic household projects. He wanted to paint a map of the world in the bedroom. He was designing a dumbwaiter that could be hung from the banister so they wouldn't have to go up and down for brandy. Since his swimming pool accident, he'd been overcome with a burst of creativity. In this same spirit, Charlotte had surprised even herself by hanging wind chimes from the front of the house. And there they were now, fidgeting in the wind, making surprisingly composed music.

And just like that, it all seemed magical again, all the banalities of a house and a life in America—the hot clean steam of the dishwasher, happy photos on the fridge, the ants running along behind the caulked seam of the backsplash, the inevitable bruised banana in the fruit bowl. She felt, for maybe the first time ever, completely unskeptical. Perhaps life was all right. Life did not forsake you completely. It did not leave you completely orphaned. He had emerged from the swimming pool, he had survived, he would be right there, in that yellow house, paying out a length of string over the banister, a pencil behind his ear.

"Clarkie!" she called, opening the door. "I'm home!"

She scooped the mail up with one arm, peeled off her high-heel shoes. In the kitchen, she dumped all the mail on the counter. In a generous mood, she took the box of chocolates she had hidden from herself out of the kitchen pantry. The chocolates waited in their little black skirts to be chosen, like fat girls at a dance. She grabbed two or three and chewed them with her eyes closed. She leaned back and shouted upstairs.

"Clark! I said I'm *home*. Didn't you miss me? Who are you talking to up there?" She swallowed, smacking her lips. She could hear pieces of faint conversation. "Clark? You on the phone?"

She brushed her hair out with her fingers, smiling. And then, somehow, the muffled sounds of the house made her frown. She went to the foot of the stairs.

"Hello?" she said.

There was no response. The talking upstairs had fallen silent. She marched up the stairs. The dumbwaiter string hung brokenly from the banister. Pushing open the bedroom door, she was surprised to find it empty. The bed was unmade, the sheets still holding the cold form of his body. Then who had been talking?

Laughing to herself, she went ahead and checked in the guest bedroom anyway. Then she checked the bathroom. Then she checked the cellar, the backyard, the pantry, the mudroom, all of the closets twice, and then returned upstairs to his little desk, the place where he read the box scores on Saturday mornings, and sat. He was not home. She ran her finger across the top of the desk and looked out the window, perplexed. The orchard, now in fruit, was occupied only by blackbirds. They flew extravagantly under the darkening sky.

On the floor of the room, she could perceive the places where other people had put their furniture. Scrapes and scars in the floorboards, and splattered paint in a corner. She saw the four ghosted feet of a desk that someone had drawn right up to the window. A glinting thing in the running board caught her eye. She went over to it and squatted. Another golden hairpin.

Standing by the window, suddenly heavy-hearted, she held the hairpin in her open hand. How many times had someone else stood here, some other woman, looking out this window into the orchard, waiting, wishing for things, watching the approach of things? She could almost feel her, feel that she was in the room with this other woman. She took a deep breath and brought her hand to her neck.

A car labored up the lane. She looked out hopefully. But only a child in the backseat stared up at the house as the car passed. The leaves of the trees outside the window began to jerk backward, and Charlotte saw that it had begun to rain again—a light, mournful, late summer rain. And, as if he had sensed the growing agitation in her mind, or had simply been flushed out by the weather, Clark leapt up from a ditch across the street in his gray sweatpants and mud boots, eating an apple.

"Oh thank God," she said.

She gasped with relief, waving, but he did not see her in the upper window.

HALF ASLEEP

And just like that it was autumn. The wind, reaching Clementine, fell slack and no longer bore the smell of fruit or brine. At night, the stars were precise. They sat fixed in lucid blackness. The maples in the yard turned yellow. The hawthorn in the back-yard dropped its purple berries in one day, its naked bark the color of old hide. In the grips of the morning chill, the house made a myriad of sounds, the cricking and cracking of the win-dowpanes and the joists.

Clark sighed and said, "I guess we should get it."

Charlotte turned her head on the pillow. "What?" she said.

"The door," said Clark. "Didn't you hear? Someone's at the door."

Charlotte raised her head from the pillow and listened. A branch snapped outside, and she heard what sounded like floor-boards downstairs creaking under the weight of a large man.

"Wasn't it just the house?" she asked. "This house makes a ton of noises. Have you noticed that?"

"No," said Clark, licking his lips. "There." He raised a fin-ger. "There it is. Didn't you hear it that time?"

"No," she said.

He went rigid in her arms and a draft came through the curtain.

"Let me go," he said. "I should go see who it is."

"No," she said. She put her head between his shoulder and neck. "Let's not get it. Let's pretend we're not home."

Clark's lips stiffened. "I don't want to pretend anything," he said. "It's the morning and it's my day off and I don't want to hang out in bed anymore."

The previous week, Clark had finally gone back to work. And as he had entered the junior high, late to the beginning of the school year, all the secretaries and Stanberry and the teachers and even the kids had smiled and looked up at his tallness with new impressionability. He found them all the more touching since he would be leaving them soon. For he still carried in him the Plan: quit, sell the house, buy a typewriter, take a chance. And it was all right, all of it, until one afternoon he found himself trying to explain to Mrs. Ormerod his heightened sense of life. How capable he felt of anything, of building a whole new life from scratch, how strong he felt. He told her about the hawthorn blossoms, beautiful white clusters in his own backyard, right there the whole time. And as he gazed fondly out the window at the school parking lot, Mrs. Ormerod had mentioned that of course such a reaction was common among those who'd experienced a brush with death. It was a rush—a death rush. A manic phase, she said, putting her plastic torso up on its shelf, a temporary euphoric high sometimes characterized by the making of grand, fantastical plans and decisions. It was, in fact, a well-documented medical phenomenon. Mrs. Ormerod slapped the eraser chalk off her hands, not realizing, perhaps, what she had done.

For just like that, the world had regained its hard edges. Down the school hallway, a phone rang shrilly, and the kids passed in their store-creased clothing. Time itself clustered back around the clock. In Clark's mind, the Plan fell apart like a house of matchsticks, a delusion itself.

Clark sat up in bed.

"Oh please," said Charlotte. "Don't get the door, Clarkie. We don't have to. Come on, let's pretend we're hiding."

She looped her arms around his waist and Clark marveled at her strength. He lay back down on the bed and tried to think of pleasant things—gravy and pecan sandies and Rod Carew and trips to the beach. But again he heard the knocking, stronger this time.

"What the hell *is* that?" Clark said, sitting up again.

"Maybe it's in your head," Charlotte murmured.

"Gee," said Clark. "Thanks. Thanks a lot."

And then, as if to bring home the very casualness with which she could say such a thing, Charlotte began snoring lightly, one finger hooked inside the band of his underwear. Out the bedroom window, he saw that the oak in the divorcee's yard was touched orange, and the blue sky turned around and around on its invisible maypole. It didn't even seem pretty to him.

Charlotte startled and raised her head and blinked against the sunlight.

"Maybe it was an early trick-or-treater," she said.

"Good Lord," said Clark, shuddering. He hated Halloween, which was fast approaching.

"I'll protect you," Charlotte said, lazily smoothing the hair on his arm.

"You'll protect me," Clark snorted. "Thanks."

But as he sat there a little longer, the wind fell still and the house itself settled, and he lay back down and sighed. Maybe it wasn't just a death rush. Maybe it would stick. Maybe tomorrow he would awake and think the sky was pretty again, and that he was indeed capable of anything, including escaping himself.

THE THING THAT HAUNTS YOU

Fear, he knew, was a relic. We inherited fear from our primitive ancestors. It had been reasonable for the ancestors to feel fear, Clark thought, for they hadn't fire or knives or glow sticks or even history. Nor did they have words. Only impulses. Run. Jump. Scream. They did not have answers, only questions: What the hell *is* that? Will it hurt? Halloween traded upon this, these leftover feelings of unspeakable ill-boding. Premonitions. Superstitions.

Clark knew he was a sucker for being afraid of Halloween. He knew Halloween was, at base, a marketing opportunity. But he had several unfortunate associations with Halloween that resulted from spending the holiday with his mother, who for several years forbade him from trick-or-treating apropos of her secret knowledge about cannibals and insane asylum breakouts. And before he could investigate this further, she stopped warning him off Halloween and dropped the whole issue. And suddenly he was allowed to go out with Mary like a normal child. But it was hard to shake the image of slobbering cannibals in the hedges, as well as the idea that he himself might be a sort of Halloween candy. And even though of course not a whit of it was true, Clark still did not like the sound of voices surrounding the house at night, and he did not like the breathless rapacity of all those trick-or-treaters. Halloween was a night of childish treachery. Kids played tricks. They threw stink bombs, toilet paper, they lit things on fire, and Clark knew that if he awoke in the morning with dog shit smeared on his stoop, his feelings would be hurt. You had to admit it, the guidance counselor was a pretty sizable target.

Daylight closing overhead, Clark drew the rake across the stiffened grass. Thick with memories, the chore was taking on a new level of protractedness. Briefly, he wondered if the yard might never be free of leaves, that he might be fated, as a character in mythology, to rake beneath an eternally shedding tree. He thought he heard, but could not be sure, a kind of ghostly music in the distance, which rose up when the wind changed directions. Honestly, who had not been somewhat frightened by Halloween as a child? And wasn't it truly kind of a scary holiday? He wondered if kids even liked it. Who hadn't burst into tears once or twice while peering through his mother's legs at a mummy that darkened the front door? Who hadn't been terrified by the shiny little witch that came out of his sister's bedroom, or woken up to find his favorite climbing tree draped with ghostly toilet paper? But then, he thought, you grow up, you see the gears and wires behind the scenery. Don't you? You saw that, of course, there weren't any deranged people loping around and bending steel fences to get at the children, there weren't any nets and there wasn't anything to be afraid of. Was there?

Clark startled at a tapping sound. It was Charlotte at the kitchen window, gesturing at him, saying something. He leaned against his rake.

"Jellybeans?" Charlotte said again to the window, holding up the package. "You bought *jellybeans*?"

Clark only stood there with his rake, squinting back. She waved him away.

"Oh forget it," she said.

She poured the jellybeans into a bowl. They weren't even orange and black. Clark walked up to the back door, blowing on his hands.

"Getting dark," he said through the screen. "I wonder if anyone will come. You know, since we're new."

Charlotte bit her lip. She wanted trick-or-treaters to come very much. She had always loved Halloween, the only night in America where one could get chocolate just because. As a child, October had seemed to her the longest month, with Halloween at the breathless end, a spasm of candy and action. It had been many years since she had celebrated Halloween. After all, she was a grown up, and she was childless. She was constitutionally incapable of being cute and engaging in cuteness, and she suspected she never was cute, even as an infant, and thusly she was a bit skeptical of the impulse that made her want to celebrate Halloween now, with decorations and all, because for whom were all these things intended? Herself? Up and down the street, she heard pots banging, a child being called for, a pogo stick—sounds of normality and domestic concord. She looked back at the jellybeans.

She said, "We can't pass these out."

"What? Why not?"

"They're not individually wrapped."

"They have to be individually wrapped?"

"Yes," said Charlotte. "Yes they do. I mean, everybody knows that."

"I didn't know that," said Clark.

"Exactly," said Charlotte.

She poured the jellybeans back into the package. She went out to the front porch and took down the glowing paper skeleton she had hung there only hours before.

"Oh come on," Clark said, pursuing. "It's just candy."

"It's not just candy," said Charlotte. "It's Halloween."

"What does it matter?"

Charlotte turned to him, pointing. "You got the wrong stuff on purpose."

Clark opened his mouth and laughed. "What? Are you kidding?" He followed her into the kitchen, and watched her untie her apron, which she hung with finality on its hook. "I didn't get the wrong stuff on purpose. Listen, the truth is I never really celebrated Halloween as a kid. I'm not used to it. I don't like it." He plucked the front of his shirt. "It scares me, all right?"

"It scares you?"

Clark looked outside. The backyard was already completely dark. Through the picture window in the living room, he could see the small figures gathering, wearing masks and pointed hats.

"My mother used to tell me that all the people in the insane asylum developed superhuman strength on Halloween. Then they'd break out of their cells and wander around, hungry for flesh."

"Hungry for flesh," said Charlotte.

"Yeah," said Clark. "They had to be fetched up one by one with special nets. I always wondered why she let Mary go out with Dad, if that was the case. I'd sit with her, in a panic, until they came home." He leaned against the counter, looking once again outside. "I guess it sort of . . . stuck with me."

"Clark," said Charlotte, standing across the counter from him. "You know that's not true, right? It's a crazy, made-up story."

"Right," he said.

But just then a young man dressed entirely in white broke through the hedges of the backyard, and Clark's first thought was, *cannibal!* He backed away from the window, while the young man, a ghost lost on his way to a party, waved in apology.

"Clark," said Charlotte. "Come on now. We're perfectly absolutely safe in this house. Your mother was just . . ." she made a frustrated gesture with her hands, ". . . confused. Come on. You really should try to forget all that."

But just then, there was a rapping on the door. They both turned and looked.

"That's funny," Charlotte said. "I just turned off the porch light."

She turned back to Clark. He was biting the side of his hand. The sight of this alarmed her. She went to the door, where the knocking persisted. Smiling demonstratively, she flung it open. But then she gasped, for the two figures standing in the darkness rather frightened her—a wild-haired teenage girl with plastic fangs and a child in a scuba suit and mask. It seemed momentarily like some sort of absurd holdup. The girl had whiskers painted on her face and two ears stuck out of her black hair, and the child could be heard breathing doggedly through a hose. The girl spat her fangs into her hand.

"We were about to *leeeeave*," squealed the girl.

"I'm sorry. We don't have any candy," Charlotte said politely. "No lights, no candy."

But then she heard Clark come up behind her.

"*Judy?*" he said. "Judy and James Nye?"

"You got it!" sang the girl. Then she threw down her pillowcase full of candy and spread her arms. "Ain't I a lulu?"

"Oh," said Charlotte. "*Oh.*"

"You guys scared the pants off of me," said Clark. "I thought—" he looked to Charlotte. "I don't know what I thought."

Judy relaxed her arms and said, looking fiercely at Clark. "It's been *too* long, Mr. Adair. May I give you a hug?" The girl pressed her head into Clark's shirt and shut her eyes. Then she gazed at Charlotte.

"Is this your wife?" she said.

"This is Charlotte."

"Hi," said Charlotte.

"May I hug you?" asked the girl.

"Oh," said Charlotte, flinching, "I—" But suddenly the girl-panther was upon her, making a purring sound. She burrowed her face in Charlotte's armpit.

"You smell good," Judy murmured.

When the two adults and two children were again facing one another in the doorway, Clark put his arm around Charlotte and gave her a squeeze. To the children he said, "You know, I've been looking for you in school, James. Where you been? Have you been a good kid, coming to school every day?"

"He's so little you can hardly see him," said Judy.

Clark knelt and put his face close to the boy's mask. Inside the mask swam the boy's blue eyes. One rubber fin squeaked against the doorstop. The boy lifted his mask, revealing a dark, rumpled head. When he looked at Clark, a grin spread unbidden across his face. Charlotte looked away. She looked back. So this was the child.

"Gimme five," said Clark.

The boy gave him five.

"Give me ten." The boy gave him ten.

"All right," said Judy. "Are you ready for your surprise?"

"Surprise?" said Clark.

"Jimmy," said the girl. "It's time."

The little boy disappeared into the darkness. He came back tugging on one end of a frayed rope. The other end of the rope led back into darkness. There was the sound of toenails coming up the flagstone. An animal sigh. Then, out of the night, wolf white eyes flashed. A pink snout nuzzled a leaf.

"Tecumseh," whispered Clark.

"Are you kidding me?!" Charlotte cried, clapping her hands. "Is this for real?"

The dog lifted his head, then perfunctorily wagged his tail. As Charlotte and Clark fell to their knees, Tecumseh skipped right past them into the house, dragging his rope.

"Here boy!" said Clark. "Good boy!"

"Good boy! Good dog!" said Charlotte. "I can't believe it!" She turned to the children. "Where *was* he?"

"Some old guy's yard," said Judy. "Tied up to the porch. He answered to his name. So we just took a little . . . poetic license, and emancipated him."

"Well *come in*," laughed Charlotte, holding out one arm, wanting now very much to hug the girl. "Happy Halloween."

In the kitchen, Charlotte plied the girl with jellybeans.

"All right," Judy said, dumping them entirely into her pillowcase. "If you insist."

Charlotte knelt and kissed Tecumseh several times on his nose. The dog licked his nose off afterward and collapsed to the kitchen floor with a sigh. In the backyard, Clark and James were assiduously raking the leaves into a big pile. Their laughter could be heard through the kitchen window.

"Let me help you with those dishes," said Judy, tying on an apron.

"No need," said Charlotte. "Really. You sit."

Ignoring her, the girl shook a huge gob of dish liquid onto a sponge and lathered it up. They stood next to each other, looking out into the backyard.

"Leaf pile jumping," said Judy, shaking her head. "Never heard of such a thing."

"Oh it's something Clark used to do with his dad when he was little."

"Jump into piles of leaves? Didn't he have *toys* or anything?"

Charlotte laughed. She had to admit that Judy Nye seemed like a normal kid, if not a little awkward with her thick conjoined eyebrows and chipped nail polish, but finally not much different from any other young girl who hoped life would turn out to be fun and pretty. Judy's hair was huge in the kitchen light, and Charlotte thought of herself in high school, loping down the gymnasium floor with a basketball while the burly gym teacher shouted, full of male grief, "*Bounce* it, you've got to *bounce* it!"

Judy pulled the crystal candy dish from the soapy water, and held it precariously with one hand. Her eyes grew wide.

"This," said the girl, "Is the prettiest thing I have *ever* seen."

"It was a wedding gift. An aunt or something," said Charlotte. "I don't even remember."

The girl turned it around in her hands.

"Careful," said Charlotte, taking the dish out of the girl's hands. She dried it off with a towel. When she turned back, the girl was looking at her, her head tilted almost to her shoulder, as one looks at a painting.

"You have the most beautiful house and the prettiest things. You must wake up every morning and praise God."

"Well," said Charlotte, replacing the dish on the shelf. "That's very sweet of you. But I don't think that God is to thank for everything. I've seen pictures of space and it sure looks spacious."

"But *I* think Jesus Christ Son of God is up at the very tippy-top of the darkness, sitting there on a plank. Sitting there looking down very quietly." The girl rinsed a plate under the tap. "Watching over you. Making sure you're all right."

"Well," said Charlotte. "That sounds nice."

The girl flipped her coarse hair back over her shoulder, and dove back into the soapy water. "So," she said. "Do you have brothers and sisters, Mrs. Adair?"

"No."

"You don't?" said the girl. "You were an only child? What's *that* like? All the candy for yourself?"

"Yes," said Charlotte, looking down. "All the candy for yourself."

"I guess your parents loved you so much they didn't need any more. What do they do, your parents? Where did you grow up? How do you get your hair so straight?"

"Listen," said Charlotte, going back over to the cupboard. "Why don't you take this candy dish? As a present from us. For finding Tecumseh." She pushed the glittering dish at the girl. "Really. It's the very least we can do. Would you please? I'd like you to have it."

The girl pursed her lips with emotion. She took the dish. "Wow," she said.

"Well, thank you again," Charlotte put her hands in her pockets. She shrugged, and looked outside. "So why don't you just sit here and relax? Have some jellybeans. I'm going to go get ready for bed. OK?" As she left the kitchen, she saw the girl with the dish under her arm, studying the photographs on the fridge. Her stare was once again keen and appraising and somewhat invasive. Upstairs, undressing in her bedroom, Charlotte could almost feel the girl's gaze pass down her body.

Something brushed against her legs.

"Oh Tecumseh," she whispered, kneeling to where the dog sat, looking up. "Were you scared? All alone. All alone in the world. The worst thing."

The dog got up and settled in his corner of the bedroom.

"All right," Charlotte said, smiling. "You win. You can sleep in here."

She went to the back window, brushing her hair. Outside, in the moonlight, Clark and the boy stood together in the yard.

The leaf pile was enormous. Surely the biggest in history. It looked like the conning tower of a great submarine surfacing in the yard. As Clark and the boy backed up against the hedges and sized up their project, Clark whistled with admiration. It had been years since he'd made a leaf pile, since boyhood. He used to wait on tenterhooks until his father said it was time, and they'd go forth into the autumn yard together with rakes. And now it was dark and moonless and it was Halloween but Clark was not afraid. James was at his side in the darkness. Being out in the night with him was like being underwater with him. No words were exchanged, but Clark felt common notions flit between their bodies like tiny birds in a chute. He noticed the silhouettes of his wife and Judy in the upstairs and downstairs windows. In the distance, the ghoulish music warbled, silly and cheap. The wind died down and the hedges behind them were quiet with anticipation. Leaves blew darkly across the crest of the pile.

Suddenly he remembered his mother pulling him away from the window. Her cold fingers, then the desperate embrace. *Don't stand by the window!* she cried. *They can reach right through!* Now, the hedges fingered his back. He pictured the deranged cannibals hiding inside them, along with the blackbirds and the ghouls and all the other monsters, and he saw that maybe fear was not the point. Maybe the point was, sometimes the thing that hunts you is as lonely as you are.

A LIFE WITH DRAGONS

That night, Clark and the children had sat up in the kitchen talking of movie stars and schoolyard injustices and laughing. Watching them unravel and eat their candy piece by piece, Clark felt rather full of guidance now that he was in his own house and had no party line to tow, and he enjoyed taking their ill-formed prejudices seriously. He did not tell them to conserve their candy. They took turns flipping jellybeans into the air and watching Tecumseh snap them out of the air.

The little boy pounced on the counter, imitating some kind of animal. He panned his head around, tongue out.

"A snake?" said Clark. "A chameleon?"

Judy ate a jellybean. "He's never seen one of those. Never been to the zoo. Not that I remember," she said.

"You should absolutely go to the zoo," said Clark. Suddenly, as he said it, it seemed a matter of the utmost importance. The zoo was good for a child's imagination, with all those rare creatures, monkeys that cried like kittens, birds with such plumage they had to lug it across the ground like magnificent traveling cases. It cheered him up, just to think of it. "What if I took you? Tomorrow."

The boy slapped the side of his head with glee. Judy bit her lip and smiled. They looked almost too happy to accept.

"I mean, would your dad mind if I took you guys to the zoo?"

Judy frowned and wagged her head. "Daddy's *very* secure," she said.

Clark saw that Judy enjoyed making mention of her father whenever possible. From her adoring reports, Clark gathered that the mysterious Mr. Nye was a real estate prospector or some kind of traveling entrepreneur, and the mother was long dead and neither child seemed curious or sad about her. They lived in a plain but very clean trailer on the outskirts of Clementine and Judy did the cooking and cleaning while he was gone, but when he returned they stayed up all night talking and Judy was allowed to have beer and once her dad had brought her a Mexican dress with blue rickrack and pretty soon they were going to move out west and sit outside all day holding aluminum sun reflectors. But he definitely had the sense of them as left alone to raise themselves, and this they simply took on the chin.

"The zoo it is," Clark said. "Tomorrow."

"But Mr. Adair," Judy's face fell. "Tomorrow's a *school* day."

From his desk in the guest bedroom early the next morning, Clark wondered what sort of role model he was to try to pass a forged note off on Gordon Stanberry. *Please excuse my son from school today . . .*

"What are you doing?" Charlotte stood in the doorway,

dressed for work. She was smiling and brushing her hair. "The Muse calling?"

Clark looked down at his letter. He saw that he had even tried to disguise his own writing into the blockish, unschooled script he imagined for Mr. Nye. He looked up at Charlotte. She looked cheerful and well rested and perfectly available to be told anything. She blinked at him prettily.

"What's that you're writing?" she asked. "Is it for me?"

Clark shrugged and put the note in his pocket. *Please excuse my son from school as he isn't feeling well.* He did not want her to tell him what he already knew: This was a vaguely crazy, vaguely unreasonable thing to do. For he had promised to be normal. He gave Charlotte a kiss, and she looked at him inquiringly.

"It's nothing," he said. "Just a silly little thing."

At school, he folded the note quickly and slipped it under Stanberry's door. He ran across the parking lot with his coat in his hand and laughter in his throat. He didn't care. It was crazy, but it made him happy to run. He was playing hooky. He could see James and Judy waiting at the edge of the parking lot, hiding behind a car. As he crossed the outer basketball court, they stepped out to the open and watched him run.

They had fun at the zoo. The kids shrieked and swatted at each other and ate cotton candy. The last exhibit they came to was the orangutan. The orangutan lived on a raised concrete platform with some palm trees on it, separated from the onlookers not by a cage but by a dry moat. The children clapped and hollered and tried to get the orangutan's attention. With his trees behind him like set pieces, the orangutan appeared to be engaged in a silent soliloquy. He had freckled hands and bowed legs, and an orange pate like a monk's, ringed with hair. In fact, he looked very much like a furry orange man, with the same longing and the same sense of destiny. Seeing him standing on a concrete platform with no privacy left a particular guilty feeling in Clark.

After chewing meditatively on his hand, the orangutan paused, as if something had just occurred to him, and turned his head.

"Look!" Judy said to Clark. "He's looking at you, Mr. Adair."

"What?"

"He is!" said James. "He's looking at you, Mr. Adair."

And he was. The orangutan's thick lower lip fell open. The insides were freckled pink. He scratched himself on the nipple. Clark straightened, wondering if the other people crowding around the orangutan's pen were jealous. What was so wonderfully savage, so recognizable, about him? Well for one, he was a man in working clothes who wasn't at work. He had his jacket slung over his shoulder, and his dark curly hair, which hadn't been cut in weeks—his own working man's rebellion—was beginning to look a little wild.

Clark looked down at James and smiled. "Do you like orangutans?"

The boy's eyes were wide as quarters. "They're my favorite," he said.

"They're not your favorite," said Judy. "Your favorite is dragons."

"You like dragons?" Clark's heart flipped over in his chest. "When I was a boy, I loved dragons. I must have read a thousand books about them."

"They're not real," James said. "They won't have one here."

"Are you so sure?" Clark chucked the boy on the shoulder.

James sighed. "I don't care if they're make-believe or not," he said. "I'd still like them just the same."

With that, James turned back to the orangutan.

My God, thought Clark. It was as if a fundamental conundrum of his own boyhood had been cleared right up for him. James was right—when a boy truly loves something, maybe his love has no doubt. So what if dragons are make-believe? So what if they're not? So what if the bear of winter was a crazy story? So what if it wasn't? So what if the knockings about in the house were real? So what if they weren't? You believe what you believe, and a story is "just a story" in the same way that a fact is "just a fact." Every once in a while, someone would tell Clark to "grow up," to "face the facts." But why, when you "grew up" did you lose access to the biggest life possible, and your cherished teachings were discredited, and dragons became the most ridiculous of lies, while you kept trying to square yourself with some impossible regimen of adult disbelief? He missed them. He missed a life with dragons in it.

He watched James rub the ball of his nose. His sister had removed herself to a bench and was smiling at some boys.

"My mother believed in dragons," Clark confessed, in a low voice.

"Really? A grown-up lady?"

"Yes. She's dead now."

The boy closed his mouth thoughtfully. Then he asked, "Did the dragons kill her?"

"No. Her mind wasn't healthy. She wasn't right in the coconut." Clark tapped his head. He squatted against the rail, pressing his brow against the chipped metal. "She sure used to tell me some crazy stories though . . ." He thought of her in sunlight, gesturing mutely toward the lake and sky. Then he said, half to himself, "Who knows? I guess you could say the dragons killed her."

Clark looked back up at the orangutan. The orangutan looked at Clark. The creature reached out his cupped hand.

"What?" Clark whispered. "What in the world do you want?"

SPECIAL GLASS

One night soon after, Clark came home to a dark house. He had already taken off his jacket and crossed the room before he saw Charlotte sitting on the couch looking at him.

"Hey!" he said.

"Hey, stranger." There was a tinkling sound from the ice in her special glass. Clark turned on the light. She flinched from it.

"What are you doing?" He sat down across from her.

"Thinking," she said. "Thinking and drinking."

"Well, it's nice to do things that rhyme," he said. He rubbed his eyes.

"Where've you been?"

"I took James and Judy Nye to the Historical Society today," he said. "They loved it. They got to see pictures of their neighborhood when it was still a swamp. Turns out, this very hill was once used as an Indian lookout and for rain dances. This is sacred land. People have lived here for hundreds of years, from the Indians to the Lippets. Isn't that amazing?"

"Mm," said Charlotte.

"They used to climb up here," he looked around, "maybe right in our yard, and look out over the valley. They'd dance around and sing to the rain god." He looked at her. "Amazing, isn't it?" He stood up and walked to the window. At the edges of the yard, the darkness was gathering. "Anyway," he said. "It's good to, you know, get out of the house. I don't think it's good for a person, to just stay in a house too long. It does weird things to you."

"I don't know," said Charlotte. "I'd like a couple weird things done to me." She took a sip of gin. "We were supposed to go out to dinner tonight."

Clark turned around quickly.

"Our anniversary?" Charlotte said.

"Oh Jesus."

"Aw, it's all right." She stood up, steadied herself against the back of a chair. "Don't be hard on yourself. I never really liked anniversaries. I'm not even hungry anymore. Isn't gin made out of potatoes?"

"Damn it," Clark said. "I can't be*lieve* it." He sat down with his head in his hands, looking genuinely disappointed in himself. Then he looked up. "Wait," he said. "I've got a great idea. Do you think maybe you'd let me make it up to you? It wouldn't take but twenty minutes."

"Forget it," Charlotte said. "I don't want a great idea. I just want you. Stay. I don't want to be alone anymore tonight. You know I hate to be alone." She patted the couch beside her, missing the spot she aimed for. "You know," she said. "I thought what you were writing at your desk last week, that surprise, I thought it was for me. For our anniversary." She laughed lightly. "But you know, the truth is, I don't even like anniversaries and birthdays and any of that. It never turns out quite how you want."

Clark blinked back at her, his eyes stinging. Then he grabbed his keys from the coffee table. "I'll bring you something," he said. "You won't regret it. Twenty minutes. You just stay put." He hesitated at the door, peering upstairs. He gazed at her fondly. "Why don't you cuddle up in front of the TV? It's on up there anyway."

"Is it?" said Charlotte.

Charlotte watched the closed door for a while. Her mind was completely empty. In fact, she had a trapdoor in the back of her head and all the cruddy mediocre thoughts had fallen out an hour ago. Jealous and lonely thoughts. Each afternoon for two weeks, he'd come home smelling of some adventure—popcorn, horses. She had been invited once or twice, but had declined, secretly hoping for a second, overwhelming invitation to prove she was really wanted. She ran her tongue over her gin-fuzzy teeth. Tecumseh entered, clicking across the floor to his spot in the corner. She admired the dog's talent for showing up only after the smoke cleared, and was once again grateful for his animal company and even his moody sighing. After a minute or so, she became aware of the sound of the television upstairs. She could not remember having turned it on.

"Silly," she said to the dog, standing. She grabbed her special glass with one hand and the bottle with the other, using them to balance while she put on her slippers. She climbed the creaky stairs and swung around the banister, spilling a little gin on the landing. As she squatted, mopping it with the hem of her robe, she heard distinctly a queer sound—the sound of a woman laughing. The laugh was long and solitary, accompanied by the sound of the bedsprings creaking.

"All right. Now cut it out," said a man's voice.

"But it's *funny*."

"No. It's not funny. It's sad. Stop laughing. You're drunk."

Charlotte stood. She screwed her face. It did not sound like the television at all, but like actual, human conversation, right behind the bedroom door.

"Hello?" said Charlotte.

Footsteps again crossed the floorboards and suddenly Charlotte found herself pressed against the wall of the hallway, hugging her bottle of gin. She looked around wildly. Was this not *her* house? Her heart pounded, the darkness of the hallway stretched in both directions. Through the door, she heard further indistinct conversation, and then the man's voice, briskly, "Come on now. Let's put on your nightshirt."

"Upsie-daisy," said the woman.

Again, the bodies on the other side of the door moved. Charlotte stared in horror at the crack in the door. She took one step toward it, hand stretched out. Blinking woozily, she moved closer.

"Oh my darling," said the woman's voice in a whisper. "How I love you."

"Yes, especially when you're drunk."

"No, all the time. I love you all the time. Forever. When you leave me, I won't even be angry with you."

"Shhhh. Raise your arms. There you go. There's my girl. There's my silly girl. You know I love you too."

"All the time?"

"All the time."

Charlotte was now standing at the door, eyes wild. She faced the crack in the door, and put her eye to it. She could see only a sliver of the room, though she swore she could hear—right there on the other side of the door—the sound of two live people breathing. Then all at once she shoved the door open, leaping backward against the banister as if from some horrible brightness.

She heard her own cry fade, and lowered her arm from her face. But there, in the bedroom, was no one. The bedroom was shadowed with the blue evening. The bedspread glowed white, and the television flickered mutely on the dresser.

"Charlie!" Clark hollered from downstairs. "I'm home! I got takeout from Happy Palace. All your favorites. Everything you like. With extra duck sauce, since I know you eat it plain. Charlotte?"

Clapping her hand to her mouth, Charlotte ran from the room. In the hall, still clutching her drink, she doubled over and heaved.

"Charlotte?" Clark came to the foot of the stairs.

His shadow leapt hugely across the stairwell.

"One second!" Charlotte said. She looked down with horror at the gin glass, smudged with fingerprints.

In the bathroom, she dumped the contents of the glass down the drain. She dumped the contents of the entire gin bottle down the drain. Then she thrust the glass into the garbage can and it landed with a crash. She pointed one finger at herself in the bathroom mirror.

"Drunk," she said, pointing. "Crazy. Ridiculous."

"Charlotte?" said Clark, leaning up. "Everything all right up there?"

"Yes," said Charlotte, wiping her mouth and stepping onto the dark landing. "Everything's perfectly fine."

NUDE TRAVEL

They sat in the living room on either end of the sofa, like ballast. Clark was reading the newspaper and Charlotte was pretending to read a book. She raised her head at the merest noise, and kept looking toward the stairwell. Finally she put the book down and folded her hands and just sat there, blinking out at the daylight.

"So," she said. "How are you, Clark? How's life?"

Clark looked up from his book. "How am I?"

Charlotte nodded.

"I'm fine," said Clark, taking a bite of toast.

"Good. It's a nice day. Isn't it?"

Clark smiled, then looked down at his paper, chewing. After a moment he dusted off his hands and stood. Charlotte stood also.

"Going somewhere?" she said.

He squinted at her. "The *kit*chen," he said. He shifted his weight.

"I'll join you," said Charlotte, glancing back over her shoulder, as if she might see another woman in a bathrobe sitting in the chair she had just vacated.

In the kitchen, she leaned against the counter, watching Clark drink an entire glass of orange juice. She knew she was behaving strangely, but she couldn't quite shove out the words: *Somebody else was in here last night.* She laughed aloud, realizing just how crazy that would sound. She looked down at her bare feet. She tried to think of something else to say.

"Oh gosh," she said at last, remembering, "The funniest thing happened the other day. I was going through the mail, and I saw this magazine with a photograph of a couple on the front. The couple was sitting on a beach. I said to myself, there's something weird about this photo. And I looked a little closer, and it turned out, they were naked! Too far away to see, you know, the specifics. The magazine was called *Naturally: Nude Recreation Travel.* Can you believe it?"

Clark blinked. "What did you do with it?"

"Well, I threw it out. Somebody must've gotten your name from some list, because it had your name on it. Can you imagine, a whole magazine devoted to nude travel? I've never heard anything so silly."

"I ordered it," said Clark. "It came free with *National Geographic.* Well, you could pick a free magazine off a list."

Charlotte put a lock of hair in her mouth. "You what?"

"Why did you throw it out? It had my name on it."

"I . . . I didn't realize you had an interest in nude travel. I thought it was safe to assume . . ."

"Don't assume." Clark turned to the sink and dumped the last bit of orange juice out. "It's actually very interesting. The relation between naturism and nudism. It's not about sex. There's not even any nude photographs in the magazine. It's a family publication."

"Those people were naked on the cover."

"You said yourself they were too far away to see anything," Clark folded his arms over his chest. "I just thought it was interesting. That's all. I was trying to be open-minded. I was trying to open my mind. Do you think I want to be a junior high school guidance counselor forever and live here and always do the same things forever? I want to be open-minded. I want to be free. I want *possibilities*."

"I didn't mean to upset you. I . . ." Charlotte swallowed. "I'm sorry," she said. "I'm sorry I threw out your magazine."

"It's all right."

Clark reached in the cabinet and took down a jar of cocktail olives. He unscrewed the jar and sniffed inside.

"That's a weird thing to eat," said Charlotte.

"Me weird?" he said. "You're the one who followed me into the kitchen." Clark sighed heavily, and then waved his hand. "Listen, Charlotte. Is everything all right? You're so *jumpy*—"

As if on cue, Charlotte screamed. She pointed toward the back door. Clark spun around to look, upsetting the glass by his hand. The glass shattered on the kitchen floor in a hundred tiny shining pieces. In the back doorway was the head of a boy, peering in. The boy waved.

"Hey, Jimmy!" said Clark. "Hold on a second!"

Clark turned to look at Charlotte, whose hand was pressed to her heart.

"Jesus, Charlotte," he said. "It's just the kid. I told him I'd take him to the park today to feed ducks."

They looked down at the glittering floor.

"Can I please come with you?" Charlotte said.

"To feed the ducks? That's not quite your thing. Is it?"

Clark lowered his eyes. Then he reached out his hand.

"Come," he said. "You can come."

But there in her own kitchen, in a field of shards, she was stranded.

BOUNTY

Clark stopped and rolled away.

"Damn," he said. "I don't know what to say."

"It's all right," Charlotte said, pulling up the bed sheets over her nakedness. The morning sun lay in stripes across her skin. "Don't say anything." She looked out the window. The trees were totally bare by then. She reached for her robe, but it was not there.

"Damn it," she snapped, surprising even herself. "Did you take my bathrobe?"

"No," he said.

She looked at him.

His eyes widened. "I swear, Charlotte."

She lay back down, closed her eyes. "I can't find my pearl necklace either. I spent an hour looking for it yesterday."

"I'm sure it's around here somewhere." Clark picked up his new *Naturally* and began to thumb through its jam-sticky pages.

"Do you think someone could have stolen it?" said Charlotte. "My necklace?"

Clark put down the magazine. "Who?"

"No, never mind. I don't know."

Charlotte looked out again at the gray treetops. In this, the deep of November, she could see clear to the next town. If only spring would hurry up and come again, she thought, so she could not see so far. In the wind, the house made its creaking sounds like a ship.

"Do you want some jelly toast?" she asked him.

"No thank you."

"You've been eating too much junk. You've been eating like a teen. When's the last time you had a leafy green? I made you pork chops last night—your favorite—but you weren't hungry." Shivering, she burrowed away from him. After a moment, she raised herself up and said, "Does anyone find it peculiar, you spending all this time with those kids? Is it wise, Clark? I mean, what does Stanberry think?"

"I'm a guidance counselor. I'm supposed to give guidance. I'm sure that Stanberry thinks I'm doing my job. Besides, I like being with them and they like being with me. They think I'm pretty damned interesting."

"All right. Don't be so defensive. I'm just asking. We're just lying here, so I'm striking up conversation."

"You want to have sex? You want to send another million sperm into obscurity?"

"What?" Charlotte clawed the hair off her face. "*What* did you say?"

"Leafy greens," muttered Clark. "Poor kid has to take care of her brother when she can hardly take care of herself. Fifteen years old and nobody cares about her. You should understand how that feels better than anybody." He looked her straight on.

"But you don't know anything about them. Who *are* they?"

"They're children. *Children*. Besides," Clark said to the ceiling, "I don't care what other people think. So I take James home after school every once in a while. So what?"

"The other day you took him to *our* home. I came out of the shower and he was there. Standing at the top of the stairs. You don't think maybe . . . he took anything?"

"You sound so jealous."

"Jealous! It's creepy, having this child around all of a sudden. And he hardly speaks. Once I caught him in the yard talking to some birds. Talking, like conversationally. I asked him if he was talking to the birds. He said, 'No ma'am. I'm talking *back*.' Why would I be jealous of a child like that?"

Clark rolled over on his back.

"I'm often jealous of children," he said. "I wish that I could go back in time. Go back into the past and retrieve something."

"What in the world would you retrieve?"

"I don't know." Then he said, "Bounty."

"Bounty," she said.

"Possibility. Innocence. Amnesia. I don't know. Sometimes I'd like to let go of all these heavy adult things—problems and history and disappointments and things, and be reborn into bounty. Back to the wide open."

Charlotte swallowed.

"I don't think we are born into bounty," she said.

"Well that's one big fat difference between you and me." Then Clark looked over at her, and softened. Her eyes were fluttering, lost. "Aw, come on. I don't mean to be harsh. It was just something to say."

"Our marriage?" she said. "Is that one of the heavy things? Do you sometimes wish you weren't married to me?"

"Oh come on, Charlotte. Don't make an issue out of this. It was an innocent thing to say. It was about me."

"But—" she gasped, and just as quickly felt ashamed, for she had no real objection. "I just don't trust them," she said.

"If you spent some time with us, you'd trust them. You'd see how great they are. But you're always begging off. When did you get so busy at work? Was there some sweatshop fire I haven't heard about?"

"I stay late at work because I don't want to be alone in the house. I get . . . frightened alone in this house."

She rolled over, cold, and put her feet on the floor. She wanted to tell him about the laughter in the guest bedroom. She wanted to tell him she was terrified of hearing the laughter again. But it was crazy. And she didn't want to leverage all her credibility that way. He did not believe her even now, about the robe and the necklace.

"Never mind," she said. "I don't know what's going on anymore. I guess I can't trust myself."

Behind her, Clark rubbed his nose slowly and then folded his hands over his chest. His face assumed a soft, rather philosophical expression.

"Maybe, Charlotte, you should consider confronting your demons."

Charlotte turned and opened her mouth. "Me confront *my* demons?

"For example," said Clark, rolling up onto his elbows. "Why do you hate kids so much?"

Charlotte looked at him. "Who me? Hate kids? I love kids."

"No you don't. Why do those little kids scare you? Why don't you ever want to have children of our own?"

"You're just trying to get out of the hot seat!"

"Probably," he said. "But I'd like to know."

Charlotte looked at him, blinking rapidly.

"I don't know," she said. "I don't know."

"Well, think about it," Clark said, not unkindly. He lay back and looked up at the ceiling. "I'd like to know what we're so afraid of." They lay there breathing beside one another. He opened his hands. "I mean, what is it?" he whispered.

After several minutes of silence, he reached over and stroked her hair. The motion was so tender and disarming that a tear fell across the bridge of Charlotte's nose and landed on the pillow.

"Oh, Charlie," he whispered. "Doesn't it ever get lonely, just you and me against the world?"

"There is no 'world'," said Charlotte, wiping her face with her wrist. "There's just a bunch of separate people."

IT BURIES US

Out of the air, out of the breadth of December, the first flake squeezed itself into being and tumbled out of the sky.

"Snow," said Clark, looking up.

"Snow!" said Charlotte, taking off her pompom hat. "Our first snow at Quail Hollow."

The flakes chased one another out of nothingness, little white jots, like ashes of some extinguished star. The snow had not been forecasted, and brought no noise and no ceremony. It fell as precisely as a cat steps. And then it was everywhere, collecting in the dimples of the trees and blanketing the grass.

Charlotte stepped into the street and looked down the hill at the town. The spires of churches were already frosted white. She could see, even from there, the green glowing face of the clock at the center of town. Above, the sky in the valley had become gray, exactly the color of the naked treetops, which made the earth and air fuse along the horizon. The streetlights had the look of lanterns, each with an orange gloriole that caught the motes of snow. She wished very much that she could stop time in order to see the snow idle in the air. She wanted to see the flakes hesitating under the lights that way, over the ground, like a good idea that takes its time in coming to mind.

"Look," she whispered.

Clark wrapped her in his arms. He opened his mitten, and they watched as several flakes fell upon the wool and melted.

"I hope it snows forever," said Clark. "I hope it buries us."

"When I was a girl," Charlotte said, "I used to dress for snow, thinking if *I* were ready, it would come."

Clark put his chin on her shoulder. "The summer that Mom, Dad, Mary, and me lived in Florida, the kids there used to ask me about snow. 'What do you mean it doesn't taste like anything,' they used to say. 'It's got to have a taste.' They were very upset. They also thought snow was alive. They thought you could keep it in a jar, like fireflies."

Below them, at the foot of the hill, two bundled figures ran across the highway and turned up the road. One figure had a sled.

"Ha," said Clark, "They're going to sled down our street."

"That's nuts," said Charlotte. She shifted in his arms. "Daddy Gagliardo used to take me to the city park when I was very young, right after they brought me home to live with them. I liked going over the little wee hills, thud thud thud, that big funny man chasing after me with his dress coat on."

The snow was coming down at a slant by then. White currents were whipped up into the darkness, then backslid to earth. The silence of the snowfall was now joined with the scraping of shovels. Busy voices from somewhere on the other side of the orchard. It was difficult to locate the sources of sounds, which was why, until the children were yards away, they did not hear them calling, *Mr. Adair! Mr. and Mrs. A!*

The smaller figure, dressed in ski pants, slid a foot or so down the hill before the other helped him to his feet. Neither of them wore boots.

"I know it looks crazy, us coming here in a blizzard," shouted Judy when she was in earshot, pulling a balding scarf from her mouth, "but crazier things have been done."

"Maybe one or two crazier things," laughed Clark.

The little boy took off his Steelers knit hat. A small plastic sled was tied to his wrist like a pet.

"Hello again," said Charlotte.

"Hello again," said the kids.

"Look at it," said Clark. "Isn't it gorgeous?"

They all turned and looked back down the hill at the snow, falling over the town. The sky was titanic. Streams of taillights went out of town in glowing red lines.

"Sometimes," said James, "it would snow and snow without stopping. The settlers had to eat dried berries and cracked-up corn."

Clark smiled down at James, who was loosely reciting information from the Historical Society. He put his hand on the boy's head. "That's right," he said.

"We were sitting around doing nothing," Judy said, "and me and Jimmy decided to get back to our roots. You know, get out in the snow."

"Your roots are in the snow?"

"We've got Eskimo blood," said Judy.

"You haven't even got boots on."

A gust stormed up the hill and pressed against their chests. "What?"

"You haven't even got boots on!" cried Charlotte again. "I don't know if it's a good idea to go sledding without boots!"

"Oh, we aren't going sledding for *fun*," Judy replied. "We came to give you another surprise."

"What?"

"A present!"

"Come inside," shouted Clark. When they moved, they left black footprints.

As the children sat drinking Swiss Miss, the snow worsened. A plow labored up the road, its headlights beaming in the dark afternoon. Noses were running. James had stopped to fish the marshmallows out of his chocolate, and Judy's head was a horrendous federation of hairs, making her look, as she peered into her cup, like a child clairvoyant.

"It'll stop any minute now," said Charlotte.

"I don't want it to," said James. "I don't want to go to school tomorrow."

"James," Judy whined. "Have some respect for Mr. Adair, would you? Dang. It's almost Christmas vacation anyway."

"Oh," said Clark, looking up. "I'd love a snow day. I'm counting the days 'til Christmas vacation."

"See? See?" said James.

"Well, I'm perfectly happy to go to school." Judy wiped her hands against her jeans, and withdrew a plastic bag from the chest of her parka. "So," she said. "Now, we just came over from Granny's—"

"She knits," said James.

"—who knits, and—"

"I didn't know you had a grandmother here," Clark said. "You never mentioned you had a grandmother here."

"She knits," said James.

"Knits and bakes."

"She bakes *a lot*."

"So we asked her a couple weeks ago, Granny, we've got this friend we'd like to give something to, the man who saved Jimmy's life, remember from the paper? And she said, don't say another word! I'm going to knit that man the handsomest sweater in the world! And when I saw it I said, you've done it, Granny! That's *him*. Merry almost Christmas."

Judy passed Clark the bag. His eyes moistened when he saw it, wrapped in a grocery bag thin and wet with snow.

"Just open it," said Charlotte. "The snow."

The children turned to look out the window, and thrilled now by the danger they cried, "Open it! Just open it!"

Clark took the sweater out of the bag.

It was a handsome sweater. It had suede patches on the elbows of the long, long arms, and was made of wool the color of alfalfa.

Charlotte gasped, about to cry out in confusion, for it had a tag on the inseam, when Clark said, "I love it. I'll never take it off. I'll even wear it in the shower."

"Don't wear it in the *show*er!" cried the children.

"Well how else will I get it clean?"

"Take it to the *laundro*mat!"

"But how will I fit my whole body into the washing machine?"

He put it on, striking affected poses while the children laughed.

"That could keep you warm in the freezo-sphere," James said. "It could keep you warm in an ice cube factory!"

Judy stood. "Well. It looks sorta bad out there, but we've got our trusty sleds. As they say, it's all downhill from here. Thanks for the cocoa."

She slapped her brother on the thigh. The boy's expression was one of surprise. He slid off the sofa with some reluctance, as if he'd been expecting to stay right where he was, drowsily licking chocolate from his wrist.

Clark looked out at the storm. The wind had died down, but the snow kept coming.

"It does look bad out there," he said after a moment. "I don't think it's safe to go out in this."

"Well, it's not going to *bury* us," Judy said.

"Look," said Clark to Charlotte. "You can't even see across the street."

"All right," Charlotte said. "All right." She went to the kitchen door and gathered her hair in her fist. To the kids she said, "Why don't you stay here until it clears. We'll drive you home."

"You guys," Judy said, already collapsing back onto the couch. "That is *so* nice of you."

But the snow did not stop. Well into the night, it snowed.

On the muted television, the weatherman gestured helplessly at his map. All around Charlotte, the room was quiet. The kids were asleep on the couch and Clark in his recliner. Even Tecumseh was breathing evenly under the dining room table. Only she and the weatherman remained awake. At intervals, she stole unhappy glances in the direction of the children, the sweater on her lap. She fingered the little Shand's tag on the inseam. She thought about her pearl necklace, grinding her teeth, going over and over events since Halloween. Granny, she thought, narrowing her eyes.

We don't know anything about them, came her own voice, so keen she actually heard it. *Who are they?*

They're children. Children.

Perhaps she could just check in the girl's pockets. Slip her hand in quickly to check for proof. She stood. The little boy's leg jerked in his sleep. Clark tasted his mouth and turned his head away. Leaning over the children so closely, Charlotte could see the waxy insides of their small ears, and she could smell their candy-scented breath. She reached slowly toward the girl's corduroy jacket. The house creaked around her, the floorboards and the walls, as if only groaning in the wind. But then, upstairs, the sound of feet slapped down the hallway toward the bathroom. She heard a loud, languorous yawning. A distinct belch.

She drew back, her hair on end. Tecumseh stood now at the room's threshold, ears stiff.

"Clark," she said, shaking his shoulder.

Clark raised his head, bleary-eyed. "What is it?"

"Just . . . just," said Charlotte, glancing over her shoulder. "Just wake up. Let's go up to bed. It's late."

It snowed late, late into the night. When Clark awoke, propping himself up on his elbows, he saw that snow had collected in the four panes of the windows. He turned over on the bed. He could not get back to sleep. Beside him, Charlotte was snoring, and the snow melting on the bedroom window sent shadows running down her face. He looked down into the sleeping, porcelain face. With the snow falling behind her, she looked like a figure depicted in a snow globe. And yet her body was so warm when she slept. Why, he wondered. Why this unconscious beckoning?

He smoothed a lock of hair behind her ear and she crinkled her nose in her sleep.

"Charlotte," he whispered.

He thought he might tell her, now that he knew, what he wanted. He wanted to live the kind of life safe for children. He wanted children asleep in the house, every night. His own children. He wanted to start life over like that. He wanted to be as exciting a parent as his mother but without the going crazy part. He wanted to step on children's toys in the darkness and teach them to brush their teeth and watch them descend the stairs in the morning with that wounded expression of children just waking up. He bent over her and embraced her. He shut his eyes, believing that he might be able to say all that. Then, very gently, he rolled on top of her, fully clothed in his pajamas. Underneath the blankets, he felt the shapes of hips and her legs. The bed creaked, and he paused there, propped on his knuckles.

"Mmm," she mumbled. "Maga."

He began to rock back and forth a little. He perceived a smile on her lips. He shut his eyes. The rocking was meditative, consoling, a pleasing motion, and soon dreams of lakes and swimming naked in lakes and Kiki Zuckerman and the sun on his body beset him. He ground his teeth together, turned his head away. He remembered the certain feeling of arousal that came from sneaking out of the house at night as an adolescent, how the crack of light might fall so damningly upon the empty bed, how the boyish wickedness snipped all the chaste little threads . . .

Suddenly he heard incredulous laughter below him. He looked down into Charlotte's open eyes.

"What are you doing?" she said. "You could *ask* me."

With his pajama sleeve, Clark wiped his damp forehead.

"Just—just," he said. He closed his eyes again, irritated, helpless. He was helpless against the loveliness of the feeling, of the lake, of the memory, of the desire to escape into its cool water. He tried not to feel his pajamas chafing against his body. And then he heard his name being called shrilly. *Just wait, why don't you*, he thought. For he was almost there, at the edge of it, his body falling forward, and then, there it was—*bounty*—as he broke into the cool, cool water.

He felt a soft blow on the side of his head.

He sat back heavily on the bed, blinking. "Ouch," he said.

"I said *get off*!" Charlotte shrieked. "Get off me!"

She kicked off the sheets and stood beside the bed, face stiff with rage. In the moonlight, her nightgown untwisted itself from her legs. She clapped both hands to her head.

"What were you doing, Clark? You were behaving like a machine, with no *feeling*."

"I didn't mean it," said Clark. "I guess I . . ."

"You hurt me!" She clasped herself and shuddered. She stared down at the shadowed floor. "You scared me!"

"I was . . ." his voice was hoarse, almost inaudible. "Remembering."

Charlotte looked at him, her face burning. He sat on the edge of the bed, nightshirt open, stomach pouched unpleasantly in his lap. His slackened expression terrified her.

"Damn you, then! Damn you!" she cried. "I've been pussyfooting around you for so long and all I want to do is just shake you by the shoulders. You don't *see*. Aren't you *awake?*"

"Be quiet now," said Clark. "The kids. Downstairs."

"Damn those kids!"

"Hey. Now cut it out."

"I'm sick of this! What is going *on* here?"

"Christ. Can't you keep your voice down?" He now sat facing away, speaking to the window. "I didn't mean it, all right? Don't you think this is hard for me too?"

"No. You know why? Because you get babied and coddled. Walking around in your dream world, you make nannies out of everyone. You get to make a mommy out of me after all. You know why I don't want to have any children, Clark? Because I've already got you!"

He swung his head in her direction.

"Stop it!" he hissed. "Stop. You're being extreme. Why must you always behave so extremely?"

"Because I want to give you some of my disappointment back! I want you to have to feel it too!" She clasped her hands to her chest. "I thought you would *love* me. But you're *away*. You're not here."

They heard a thump downstairs.

Suddenly, a black, winged thing fell off its branch in Clark's chest and went flying up his throat, flapping heavy and wet. The black thing closed its feathers over his mind. He climbed onto the bed and faced his wife, not two inches away, and growled, "Do you want to know the real reason why we don't have any kids?"

He backed off and his eyes shone darkly.

"I know already. It's because I said so and you agreed. You wanted so badly to get married, so quickly. You agreed to it!"

"That's not the real reason," said Clark.

"No! I won't believe you anyway! I don't believe you anymore. You're not really here. You died with your mother. Yes! You threw yourself into the grave! You're like a big floating *nothing*."

Clark began to laugh. His laughter made Charlotte uneasy. It left little gouges in the air. He himself did not know where the laughter came from nor what it portended. Someone was in the kitchen downstairs, at the sink. The sound of water. The door of the refrigerator. So late, so dark.

Charlotte trembled. "Why are you laughing?"

"Because of the reason," said Clark.

"The reason?"

"The reason we don't have kids. It's so simple. Right there in front of me the whole time. It's because your heart isn't big enough."

There was a brief, awful silence.

"No. That's not true," Charlotte said finally, her voice getting higher, "It's because I don't want to. It's because I don't want to have a hundred little yous running around."

"Your. Heart. Isn't. Big enough." He pronounced each word with this new tool of his voice. A draft from the shaking window washed over her. "Your heart's hard and small. You strangle it with your fear and—"

"Stop it!"

"—mistrust of everything."

"Just stop!" She buried her face in the pillow and cried, "Take it back!"

"No."

"Then go away! Go play with your little friends! You liar. You fool. But you better watch them closer, Clark. Because you have no idea what a sucker you are."

She raised her head and spat, "Where do think your brass bookends went and my pearl necklace and robe? They're *stealing* from us Clark. Just last week I tried to bring it up but you got angry. At *me*! I want them out of here! I want my stuff back! I want you."

"I'm not your stuff."

"Call it what you will," said Charlotte, her eyes brimming with tears. "But if we didn't really want to belong to each other, we shouldn't have gotten married."

Now Clark paused. His eyes narrowed.

"You're jealous. You're jealous of anyone who likes me. Those kids. My own *mother*."

"Your mother? Your mother was taking you down with her! She might have loved you once but then she went crazy. You have *no idea* how much your father and I protected you."

"You're lying."

"I'm not lying. Ask him! Don't believe me, go ask your father!"

"Listen," Clark put his finger in her face. "Those kids are not stealing from us. It's you. You have no faith. You can't even trust a *child*."

"That sweater! I saw that sweater she gave you in Shand's with my own eyes. Almost bought it for you myself, but it was one hundred dollars. Go see for yourself! Where does this Granny come from, all of a sudden? It's simple. You've been lied to. You keep looking so hard for someone to love you. I'm right here, you idiot!"

"I'm sick of listening to this. I'm sick of all this," Clark made an angry, generalized motion. His lips quavered. "This suffocating little house. This routine with you. Stay, sit, heel. Don't be too *different*. Don't be like *her*. I'm going to sleep in the other room."

"Just like a child. That's what I'm saying. Can't you stay here and talk to your own wife? Stay! Talk to me."

"Stay!" Clark shouted back. "Sit!"

"That's not what I *mean*."

"Are you sure?"

He got out of bed and stalked out the door, hunching over to get through the low frame. A moment later he came back in.

"Generosity!" he yelled. "Kindness! Spontaneity! Try them out sometime, Charlotte! Why are you hiding? At least with me, I'm out there in the world. I'm giving it a try. I might be a fool sometimes but I'm giving it a try. I'm not hiding in *shame* because I'm not *perfect*. Because my mommy gave me up. You're missing life. You're too pro*tec*ted." He leaned against the wall, right by the fist-sized hole in the plaster, and bent his head. "Look, Charlotte," he said, his voice quieter, "Why are you crying? You never cry. Look. I can't trust you. It feels like a trick."

Alarmed, Charlotte felt her face, which was wet. She wiped her hand slowly across the sheet.

"Your mommy gave you up too," she said, sniffling.

"I know. And you were glad. It satisfied you. I think it made you feel better."

"Not true!"

"Don't lie, Charlotte."

"But you didn't cry. You didn't even cry when they buried her."

"Yeah well," said Clark, shrugging. "Turns out, your heart breaks anyway. How could I talk to you about it? You were so unsympathetic. I know she was crazy, but she was my mother!"

And now a sob rose in Clark's throat, but he backed away from it, coughing into his fist. He stood in the doorway, blinking.

"So now you want to break my heart?" said Charlotte.

"I can't break it," he said. "I'm afraid that's true. That's what I'm saying."

"But you can break it. Please don't." She raised her arms to him. "Please come back to bed."

"I came in because I forgot my book," he said, snatching a paperback from the nightstand, then leaving again.

In another moment she saw his shadow approach in the hallway. He walked into the bedroom. She raised her arms again.

"Come back to bed, baby," she gasped. "Forgive me!"

Clark snatched his pillow from the mattress.

"I forgot my pillow," he said.

"Please!" Charlotte cried to his retreating shape, the front of her nightshirt damp with tears. "Please don't leave me here alone!"

PART THREE

FLASHES OF YOU

Charlotte sat straight up in bed, sure that her sleep had interrupted an important point she'd been making. She blinked, rolled her head around on her shoulders. Her body ached. She slapped her hand to her forehead. Outside, the light was deep blue.

"Clark?" she said. "I think I'm coming down with something."

The bathroom door was ajar. A slit of light lay against the floor. She put her feet on the floor and peered forward. The floor was cold but her feet were pulsing hot. She expected the floor to hiss where it met her flesh.

"Clark?" she said again. "What are you doing in there?" She rubbed her shoulders. "Are you flexing? I know you do that. I've seen you through the keyhole. Clark?"

She reached forward and plucked open the bathroom door. Her expectation of seeing him standing there was so well detailed that she did, for a moment, see him, flushed and hairy-legged, flexing in front of the mirror wearing his favorite T-shirt with the decal name of his boyhood baseball league fading across it. He looked at her, and then fizzled into space. The light of the bathroom hurt her eyes. Yes, she was definitely coming down with something.

She would go downstairs immediately and call in sick to work. She got up and made the bed in the tender, matronly way of sick people. She stopped and looked toward the curtains. An unspecific blue light was glowing through them. What time was it anyway? Morning, surely. There came a repetitive birdcall, high and tense, over the house. Then the noise of a banging pot, which was how the Ribbendrops called their child home in the evening. Charlotte stopped, put a hand to her throat. Had she slept the entire day?

"Clark?" she said again, pattering to the doorway. She looked both ways down the hall, but then hesitated, not wanting to leave the bedroom. "Clark, have you seen my watch?" She turned around, scanning the surfaces. Then she went to the window and pulled aside the curtains to discover that the world was entirely buried in snow.

As if to keep the outrageous image from intruding, she put both hands on the frozen windowpane. The trees outside were laden white, as if wracked by blossom, hanging without life. The nearby houses were shuttered and dark. The street had not been plowed, but there was a large dark hole in the snow just under the window. The car was gone. She blushed, feeling foolish for hollering. She thought of how much she disliked it when Clark shouted across the house. She let the curtains collapse in front of her. What had someone said about the snow? Just yesterday, was it? *Well, it's not going to bury us.*

She shuddered. A wave of nausea sent her running to the toilet.

The hole of the toilet stared back at her. Her memory rustled, heaved, and drew out of itself, like a cruel trick, the terrible argument of the previous night. She remembered the sound of her own pleading. The way his eyes stared back without love or mercy. *Please don't leave me here alone!* She remembered his overgrown shadow retreating down the hall and how she lay there sleepless and broken, listening to the sound of his snoring in the guest room until she'd gone and taken some of his sleeping pills, which had sent her this utter insentience. But the price of the insentience, the price of sleep, she saw now, was a strange and grotesque emotion that had grown in the meantime, shocking in its pureness. She clutched her stomach and heaved. But the emotion would not disgorge.

In a panic, she fumbled for a towel, soaked it in cold water, and buried her face inside. Then, looking at her bloated image in the mirror, she tried to smile. She was not to be trusted. After all, she was only coming down with something.

With some spirit, she emerged from the bathroom and dressed, deciding that it did not matter what time it was. She felt too ill to go to work, and besides, nobody could be expected to go out in this. She had never seen anything quite like it before. The houses up the street were buried to the bottom windows. Coming slowly down the stairs, she noticed that it had not grown any lighter since she awoke. Rather, the blue light was deepening, as it does at dusk. Her mind trailed somewhat behind these observations. She rounded the banister and crossed the cold, dim room, getting halfway across before stopping short.

She put her finger to her lip. What was it—the particular bareness to the room? She ran her hand across the top of the side table. Where was the silver set? Daddy Gagliardo's brass compass? The little baubles and inheritances and even, on the bare wall, the framed photograph of Clark and Charlotte embracing on the beach? She spun around, her hands going out to touch the things that weren't there. She put her hand on the wall where the photograph had hung. She turned around, turned around again, disbelieving. Dizzy, she collapsed in a chair.

And then she thought of her own captured face traveling in the lap of a small child across—where did they say they would go with their daddy someday—California? She couldn't wait for Clark to return from wherever he was, so she could gloat. She would say, See? Still think those kids are angels? Still think childhood is a bowl of cherries? A *bounty*? But instead of satisfaction at being right, she felt, against her will, the sting of envy. California. Theft. In her own shipwrecked childhood, she would never have thought of it. She would never have got her little orphan hands around such a plan of self-rescue. And they were sort of sweet to have bothered to steal the photograph. Come to think of it, she would not miss the silver set or the compass or any of the baubles and detritus that had trailed behind their lives until now like a string of tin cans. She heard a creaking sound and stood, expecting to see Clark walk through the front door in his snow boots. But the door did not open and she had to brace herself against a wall, hit with a fresh wave of nausea.

Only Tecumseh came clicking across the floor from the kitchen, whimpering. He brushed against her legs. At least she was not entirely alone. To be alone—it was the worst thing imaginable.

Outside, the dog picked his way through the snow and peed at length. Charlotte saw that above the house, a large bird was flying in great circles, making a tense, delicate call. Its white breast flashed in the dim light. She watched the bird make two careful passes over the house.

She went back inside, to the kitchen, head in her hands, where even the wall clock was missing. The countertop gleamed with its lack of appliances. Outside, the shadow of the bird crossed the hardening snow. On the kitchen table, she discovered a note, written in a black magic marker, which had been left there, to the side, as if for her to make her useless reply. She held the paper up to her eyes. It read:

Dear Charlotte,

I don't know where I'm going. I'm sorry, but I'm taking the car. Don't worry about me. I don't know what to write. I've never done anything like this before.

I saw what the kids did. They sure took a lot of stuff. So hey, you were right. That's unfortunate about the compass. The rest of it, God they can have it.

When I was little I used to think that what was right would always be obvious to me. I don't know. There's no secret buried covenant of truth or at least I don't know where the hell it is. Do you know?

I love you, but I guess you think so what?

Charlotte, maybe love just kind of rings and rings like a bell for no reason. Maybe you have to be crazy.

Your husband,
Clark

Charlotte put the note down. Suddenly she felt again that she might vomit, and she stood and walked unsteadily through the house. In each corner she passed, each room, in each doorway, for one moment again she actually felt she saw him—the flash of his eyes or pretty white teeth, the disorder of his curly hair, his body collapsed in laughter—such was the strength of who he'd been when he was there. He was her husband, and sometimes his presence was confusing, but as if she had been granted some horrible wish, she now had his absence, which was completely unambiguous.

After a while she found herself once again outside in the bracing air, standing in her slippers and nightgown on the snowbound porch, sobbing. The wind blew hollowly down the street. Up in the sky, the darkness was now dissolving the forms of the clouds, replacing them with stars. The large bird swept across her view again, lower this time.

"Go away!" she cried, waving her arms, as the bird made its wide, measuring circles. "Get away from here!"

FEVER

Several indistinct days passed and her fever grew. At first, she spent the time in front of the television in the guest bedroom. She liked the loud wheedling voices going on and on, obscuring the thumps that might have been melting off the roof but seemed in fact to be getting closer, footsteps, *in*side. Under her blanket, she clung to herself. She had stopped crying. The phone did not ring. She did not eat. She hustled Tecumseh out into the cold only to beat her return to the screaming television as soon as she could. The illness was in her joints and her stomach, but it also began to cloud her mind.

Then, in one unremarkable moment, she grew too sick to watch television, too sick to be afraid, and stepped out at last into the hallway. Into the quiet aloneness. Standing there, she felt how weakened she really was. Her bones seemed to be rotting and she could barely trust them to stand. Her skin itself felt raw and fluish and extraordinarily sensitive, as delicate as the film that forms over hot milk. She shuffled down the hall to the room she was most afraid of. There, from the doorway, she gazed at their empty bed. Sheets twisted, pillows askew—the empty stage of marriage. She lay down upon it. There at last, the fever overcame her. She wondered if the heat of her body would ignite the bed sheets. She gazed at the increasingly hazy view out the bedroom window.

Aside from being a source of true physical suffering, the fever soon began to inspire confusing thoughts—flashes, bright as day, but without context. She tossed in bed, trying to find a position that would make them cease. But in the fever's increasingly hot smear, the images arose faster, one after the other, then flew past, leaving behind them shimmering, colored trails. Nothing—mere irrelevancies, unexplained: a hat on a bed, a bandaged finger held up for inspection, a piece of kite string. The images seemed to be coming from her own mind, and yet the hat, the finger—they weren't her own. And then, as in a symphonic movement, the soft rising of the many isolated notes of the human day: a stuttered word, tuneless humming, the squeaking sound of windows being washed. Weakened, overruled, she succumbed to these things. She no longer pined for Clark, whose continuing absence made a terrible sort of sense in this heat, and when she rolled over on the bed, the sheets peeling off her like skins, she was almost glad he was not there, hogging the mattress. When, on the edge of sleep, she heard piano music coming from the other room, she felt she finally understood where she was. She was in a museum of time. She was wandering around in the museum of discarded moments— lost, loose, left memories, brief as sighs. A cloud of baking flour bloomed in the air. Spilled milk ticked off a countertop. Daffodils. Excited footsteps. The clicking of a caliper or knitting needles. The bitter smell of orange rinds. An argument about Canada. A paper airplane. A man calling *Maaaarion, Maaaarion,* very softly, as if trying to wake somebody. Charlotte felt a great tenderness wash over her. For that moment she did not care where the moments came from. They were lovely; the air was dense with them. She reached up to touch a child's mobile that was now spinning overhead. Just as she felt the satisfying roundness of the mirrored circles, the drunken laughter resounded down the hall. Glass shattered. Charlotte turned her head bitterly away.

"Leave me alone now," she muttered, turning over on the mattress. "Just go away."

But through the fibers of the pillow that vainly covered her ears, she could still hear: an amorous sigh, a jangled key ring, a struggle to lift something large. And gradually, very pronounced entire sentences: *Great, Evelyn. You throw my shoe at me and I have to go after it.* And, elsewhere, *Save some hot water for me, Manny, why don't you.* A crow yawed at the window. A pogo stick persisted in the street. *Do you love me all the time? Yes,* came the soft reply. *All the time.* A conductor's wand kept time against the edge of a piano. Out of breath now, Charlotte surfaced to see the second hand of the clock inching around the face. Beyond that, on the bedside table, the bottle of aspirin. In a moment of lucidity, she sought the bottle with her hand. Trembling, she tried to shake out a couple tablets. But none came out. She looked into the bottle, then threw it empty on the floor.

"Clark," she groaned. "Go get me some medicine. I need something for the flu."

"There's nothing you can do for the flu," said Clark, poking his head out of the bathroom. "You know that. You just have to suffer through it."

"Oh yeah?" she said. "Well, I'll make you suffer too."

"I bet you will."

"You probably gave it to me, you bum."

Clark's head disappeared behind the door.

"Oh yeah?" he said from inside the bathroom. "Then how come I'm not sick too?"

"I don't know," said Charlotte. "That's your diabolical secret."

She rolled her head on the pillow, smiled at the bathroom door.

"It even hurts to smile," she said. "Clarkie?"

She could hear the tapping of his razor against the sink.

"Come on out and fuss over me. Please? Just for a second? You always make me feel better when you fuss over me. Clark?"

"I suppose," sighed the woman, "we could always repaint."

Charlotte turned quickly. Next to her on the bed was a woman just about her own age, lying dressed, with her arms over her head. Her golden hair was bobbed and she played thoughtfully with her bangs.

"What did you say?" Charlotte asked the woman.

The woman took a lump of something waxy out of her skirt and fingered it, not responding. A tall, broad-faced man in a black turtleneck came to the doorway. He hesitated for a moment outside the room and looked in at the young woman. "Sure we can," he said gently. "We can make the best of this."

The woman said nothing, staring at her cube of wax.

"The best of what?" asked Charlotte.

"Sweetheart," the man continued, leaning against the doorway. "Why always the sad thoughts, at yourself day and night? Don't you like this house?"

"It's strange," said the woman. "I don't ever feel as if I'm alone. It's the strangest sensation." Charlotte felt the woman shudder beside her. "It's a sad house, Bobby," murmured the woman. "There's too much *caught* in it."

"Well, it's a starter home," said the man, trying to smile. "It's just for starters."

When the woman did not laugh, the man entered the room.

"I'm sorry, Marion," he said, a faint lilt to his voice. "I'm sorry I can't give you everything you want. But I love you. Couples who love each other get through all sorts of things. Why, we've only just gotten started. We're just at the beginning. Isn't that exciting?"

The woman turned her head. She and Charlotte faced one another for an instant.

"No," said the woman. "I can't feel it."

Then the man whirled around and struck the bedroom wall with his fist. He leaned back from the broken plaster, cradling his hand.

"Jesus, Marion," shouted the man, his eyes wet with tears. "Jesus, quit blaming everyone else. Don't you get it? We have to make our*selves* happy. We're the gods of our own life! We could do *anything*." He looked at his wounded hand, then he looked back at the woman on the bed. Charlotte sat up now, reaching out. "The question is," the man said, "are you brave enough?"

"Yes!" cried Charlotte. "She is. *Aren't* you—"

She turned, but the woman was no longer lying beside her. Now there was a banging on the front door that was startling, and a woman's voice screaming from the front of the house: *Jason, goddamn it, let me in. I'll stand here and scream! This whole stupid neighborhood will hear me again!* Charlotte stood up and ran to the door of the bedroom. Then the woman's voice could be heard again, more intimately, *Jason, please. I love you. Open the door.*

Now Charlotte was running down the hallway, but the hall was endless, with dozens of rooms full of people conferring and fighting and sitting in silence. Through one doorway, an adolescent girl sat at a desk, the trash can beside her filled with crumpled pink stationary. In his corner, a red-haired infant furiously rattled the bars of his crib. A young woman crossed the room, holding out a dress, saying, "I can't wait to see their faces when we tell them. Save some hot water for me, Manny, why don't you." Just then a shoe sailed over Charlotte's head and slapped against the staircase wall. She whirled around to see a middle-aged man in pleated dress pants and undershirt come out of the bedroom and stare after the shoe. "Great, Evelyn," the man muttered. "You throw *my* shoe at me and *I* have to go run after it." He turned and looked at Charlotte. "Well, is there anything else you'd like to throw at me, as long as I'm standing here?"

Charlotte steadied herself against the banister. She heard a voice, further down the hall, in faint conversation, "So now you want to break my heart?"

"I can't break it. That's what I'm saying."

"But you can break it. Please don't. *Please* come back to bed."

Cautiously, cautiously, Charlotte inched back down the hall, looking around each doorway. Could she bear to see herself as a moment—wretched, abandoned, on the bed? She turned the corner of the very room. But there, barely making a dent on the bed's edge, sat a girl of eight or nine, holding a hand mirror. With her other hand, she brushed her long, yellow hair. Hair the color of sugar corn. The brush made soft hushing sounds as she pulled it through. The girl appraised herself in the hand mirror. She flashed a crooked smile. Outside, it was raining. The silver rain filled the window. Charlotte stepped closer to hear what the girl was singing. *Oh wasn't it a bit of luck that I was born a baby duck. With yellow socks and yellow shoes so I may go wherever I chose.* Just then, downstairs, the phone began to ring. Suddenly, as if she was not sick at all, Charlotte spun around and ran down the stairs toward it.

"Coming!" she cried. "Wait! Wait!"

Dashing into the kitchen, she picked up the telephone.

"Clark!" she cried. "Is that you?"

"Is it," the voice said tentatively, "who?"

"Have you found Clark?" Now she was smiling radiantly. She looked down at the counter and her hair hung in wet, sweaty spirals around her face. This was good, she knew. She was sweating out the fever. "I really . . . need to . . . talk to him."

"No, silly," said the voice. "It's *me*."

Charlotte swallowed, breathing hard. She rubbed her eyes with the palm of her hand. Over the sound of her breathing, the regularized sound of machinery echoed through a large hall.

"*Mom*my," said the woman. "It's Mommy. They gave Mommy a little break to call you at home. 'Cause you're sick. Is Grammy taking good care of you?"

Then, as if summoned to the task, Charlotte began to cry.

"Oh sweetie," said the woman. "Don't cry. What's the matter?"

Charlotte cried now with great sobs. Tears fell on the countertop and she shook from exertion. She almost laughed. She literally could not stop herself now.

"It's all right, baby. It'll be all right," soothed the voice on the telephone. "Why don't you get yourself a washcloth and put it under the cold water. Can you reach? Yes? Put it against your face."

Trembling, Charlotte obeyed. She wet a dishrag under the kitchen faucet, and pressed it to her forehead.

"How about after you ask Grammy to get you some warm milk," said the woman. "Doesn't that sound good, Charlotte honey? Can you say 'milk' to Grammy?"

Charlotte wiped her eyes with the back of her hand and nodded. She stood listening to the voice and then she closed her eyes. She took a deep breath.

"Milk," she said.

The woman sighed. "I'll be home soon. *Very* soon."

"I miss you," sighed Charlotte.

"I miss you too, sweetheart."

"I used to think about you all the time," said Charlotte. There was a wave of static in the connection. "But I don't think about you anymore. I haven't thought of any of it in years."

Suddenly, over the sound of the machinery, came the long sounding of a horn.

"Mommy has to go sweetie."

"Now wait a minute," said Charlotte, clenching her fists. "Now hold on just one minute. Now that I've got you, I want to ask you some things. It's only fair!"

"Please don't make Mommy feel bad," chastened the woman's voice. "There's nothing Mommy can do."

"Wait!" cried Charlotte. "Hold on!"

"Mommy loves you too. Kisses."

Just then the telephone slipped out of Charlotte's wet fist. Gasping, she stooped down and pressed it back against her ear. There was no sound at all on the other end.

"Mama?" she said into the silence.

When she opened her eyes this time, there was nothing but a landscape of white fabric—the pillow, monumental to her eye. She raised her head. Tecumseh was assiduously licking her fingers. Moments before, she had pulled herself up the staircase—had she not?—strangers and faces and even a drunk lady in a clown suit making a crowded passage. Now she stared at the empty room, the empty doorway, listening. Aside from the dog's retreating steps, the house was quiet. She lay there, heart pounding, the moon hovering outside the window. An hour passed before her heart quit pounding.

Finally, she got out of bed and walked down the hallway, looking into the rooms. Inside them, chairs sat empty, the curtains hung unstirred. There was no one. She was strangely, horribly disappointed. In the stark silence of the house, the floorboards groaned under her weight. Her wet nightgown clung to her legs. The fever had drained from her body. Were they all gone now? Down in the kitchen, just to be sure, she picked up the telephone.

"Hello?" she said.

She replaced the phone to the hook.

Upstairs, she turned on all the lights. The sky outside was pitch black, and a ghost town sort of wind was blowing through the silent neighborhood. The bathroom light fell backward over the damp, rumpled bed. Stopping before the opened medicine cabinet, she took down the bottle of sleeping pills and removed the cap. Her palm was wet, and the capsule clung to it as she tried to put it in her mouth. Swallowing, she shut the medicine cabinet and gazed at her face in the trisected mirror. Behind her reflection, infinite Charlottes multiplied in the distance. Was the last Charlotte, the one too far back too see, the child who sat on the bed? She removed her soaked nightgown and stood yellow blue and human before her numinous reflections. Then she got back into bed and stared out at the moon.

It was sad, she thought, all the lost moments. How moments are endlessly forgotten, and one's life is a patchwork of holes. And love, a best guess. But your lost moments, perhaps they remember you. Perhaps they are caught in the eaves and the corners and the gutters of the lost houses. A tear rolled down the side of Charlotte's cheek. *Milk*, she whispered. She looked at the bottle of pills she had brought with her to bed. The bottle glowed orange upon the bedside table.

Here was one she had not forgotten: looking through a telescope for the first time. Looking up at the planets, as if from the bottom of a well, into the circular eye, her first thought had been *poor lonely God*. She could remember Daddy Gagliardo standing beside her, with his bland good nature trying to explain the idea that the initial explosion that created the universe was still happening, and space ever-inflationary. But even as a child, she knew what this meant—that it would only become more difficult to locate what you had lost, for the galaxy was yet breaking apart, and the stars, in their brilliant independence, were burning for no one.

Charlotte reached for the bottle of pills, which she fancied had moved, in those minutes of thinking, half an inch further away. She thought of Clark, floating backward, arms outstretched, a garden of stars in the inky black behind him. She thought of her mother, floating backward, arms outstretched. You had to hold on so tightly. The grip slips. Poor old God, who never had anybody. Or was he the luckiest? God also floated backward. In the silence, Charlotte tried to sing to herself. But her voice, tremulous and off-key, was a rusty comfort. She held the pill bottle up to the light. The night was so silent. It was easy to ask Why, but the question Why not was perhaps the better question.

And indeed, she thought, trembling and naked and cold, Why not?

OPEN SEA

Clark sat staring at the blank movie screen. In the quiet, after everyone had left, the boy with the dustpan swept around him. It was his third time seeing the same film in a row, and by then the plot of it had become familiar to him: A young priest falls in love with a girl, and in his stupid selflessness the priest sets the girl up with his brother, who ends up beating her at whim with his shoe. Finally, maddened by guilt and sexual torment, the priest comes and steals the girl away from his brother, and they hide out in a cave, where she ends up starving to death, so that the priest has to grow old in exile and is forced to tell the story over and over and over to a bunch of strangers in the Clementine Triplex.

He looked around. It was dark in the theater and the air was lurid with smells—warmed-up, florid colognes, a hash of gardenia and cedar and methyl alcohol, human gassiness, false butter, breath, the generalized wake of excited people, plus, on his own fingers, the smell of chocolate. Clark bit the white candy jots out from his nails. Reaching blindly for his soda, he knocked it over. The ice slid under a chair. He looked around for the boy with the broom and dustpan, but except for the imperious eye of the projector behind him, he was alone.

"Hey," he said, waving up at the eye. "Anybody up there?"

He thought he saw a furtive shadow in the booth.

"Hey," he called, smiling. "Some help please. I just spilled my soda."

Nobody answered, but he felt that he was being listened to. He waved. The eye blinked, seemed to calcify, and a brightness—a mechanic consciousness—came to its iris.

"Hey up there!" called Clark.

He stood and waved until he noticed a short couple, melting snow in their haircuts, each holding a tub of popcorn, hesitating in the dark aisle. Clark froze. There hadn't been more than one or two stragglers in the theater all day. The man, without taking his eyes off Clark, took a kernel from his tub and ate it.

Clark put his hands in his pockets. "Hi," he said.

The couple said nothing.

"Well, have a seat," said Clark. "We've got the place to ourselves."

"You're from the last show, aren't you," the woman said.

Clark sat down. Quietly he answered, "You're allowed to see the movie as many times as you want."

The couple settled in the middle section, half a dozen rows back.

"Crazy weather," Clark called over his shoulder. "Still snowing out there?"

"Yes and no," said the man.

After a while, he could hear them chewing.

"Was it good?" asked the man behind him.

"What?"

"The movie. Was it any good?"

Gratefully, Clark turned around in his seat. "There's this priest who falls in love with a girl—"

"Uh-huh," said the man, from the darkness.

"And of course he can't do anything about it—"

"No."

"Because he's got to be chaste. So he sets the girl up with his brother, who—" He stopped. They chewed. Did they want to hear the entire story? They both wore eyeglasses that glinted in the dark, obscuring their eyes. Up behind their heads, the eye of the camera was alert, divine.

"Anyway, the brother's a jackass, and he beats her with a shoe whenever she looks at him wrong. Finally, the priest, who's still in love with her, starts to feel so tormented, he—" again, Clark waited. How difficult, in the end, to speak with strangers! He never really knew it. He felt that he was rendezvousing with a second ship on the open sea, in a world made purely of water, and this skinny couple was on deck, inquiring of him, Do you know where the land went? What did they have in common, Clark wondered, other than the fact that they were all three alive at once?

"Finally he what?" asked the man.

All of a sudden, he wanted to get out of there. The ugliness came crashing down on him so hard he felt his shoulders ache. What had he done? What in the world had he done? How long had he been in the theater? What does "yes and no" really mean? There, in the dark, alone and attached to nothing, he wondered if his own inconsequence would make him light enough to fall off the earth. His heart dropped, then just before hitting the ground recovered itself and saw that regret was a trick, that if he was going to do this—*leave*—he would have to steel himself. He shoved her pale, tear-stained face aside.

"Hey kid," he called to the boy with the broom and the dustpan who'd begun sweeping in the back. "You, kid. Did you see me up there?"

The boy walked up to the last row of seats and put his hand to his ear. His white shirt glowed in the seamy darkness. "What say?"

"Are you the projectionist?"

"No sir."

"Could I talk to him maybe?"

"What do you want? You want to talk to the projectionist?"

"Well," Clark confessed, "I was actually just curious. If there was anybody up there or not. Just curious, really."

"What does it matter as long as it works?" crowed the woman.

"Well," Clark continued, glancing at the woman, "doesn't he have to go to projectionist school, the projectionist? You know, like a barber or a chef?"

The boy laughed.

"What's so funny?" Clark said, smiling.

The boy laughed. Then the couple began to laugh. They laughed like their throats were full of butter. Gluga gluga. In the velveteen empire of the Triplex, the laughter seemed both huge and muted, like the battle sounds of the war movie already in process next door.

"You know," said the boy, recovering, "they don't do it like they used to. You don't have some guy up there changing reels. Somebody, sometimes even the manager, sets it up at the very beginning to make sure it's in focus. Then he pushes a button." The boy was now leaning sportingly against his broom. "It's all pretty much mechanized. So there's really no need for someone up there. Give it a year or so, it'll be entirely digital. No room at all for human error. We'll just program the house and sit back all day, drinking lemonade."

Clark kicked at the ice cubes underfoot. His body was still producing a sound like laughter when, just then, as if in a gesture of encouragement to him, the eye exploded, and an enormous cone of light came out of it, with manic shapes inside and the encrypted flashings of words and numbers, too fast to believe, the scratchy, needle-on-vinyl sound, and the stark, declarative green of the screen. Later, when the lovely, unobtainable girl first appeared to the priest, carrying a bunch of wildflowers out of the vestry, even though he had seen it three times already, Clark's heart was beating hard, because there was, he was sure of it—there *had to be* a projectionist, an author, a system, an overseer, a fate, someone accountable and sorry about it, sorry about all this, this tragedy, this unanticipated complication, this saying of words with someone else's mouth, the cruelty of good people—somebody not Jesus but like Jesus, trapped inside his immortal circumstances, looking out over the world with long sadness, wishing for the good old days when men and women were simple and he himself walked undistinguished among them.

ON FIRE BUT NOT BURNING

The Clementine Motor Inn stood alone between the arcade and the freeway, awash in a pool of floodlights. Clark hesitated at the plate-glass doors, knee-high in a snowdrift. A young woman in a cheap blue suit was playing solitaire on the front desk. Behind her, a janitor leaned on a mop and stared outside.

He stepped back into the night's shadows and swore at himself. How could everything have possibly gone more wrong? His car was stuck in a ditch outside the Triplex. He was so cold that the top half of his head felt numb, and he was afraid to pass his hand over his hair in case he came across his exposed brain. Clenching and unclenching his frozen hands, he looked back toward the dim downtown with accusation. He hated the place now. Just as soon as he could, he was going to leave it for good— leave everything, for real this time, leave everything behind.

But walking back from the Triplex through the deserted streets, the town had looked so damned pretty in the snow. The traffic lights had clicked so softly in the night air. The glowing yellow umbrella of the Mini Mart was like a warm earthly star. As Clark strode across the quiet intersection, the clerk inside the Mini Mart waved him in. Clark demurred, even though he didn't even have a hat or gloves on, just the upturned collar of his coat and a pair of snow-soaked Tall Man corduroys.

But just then, arms full of candy bars, a girl had emerged, wearing a light blue parka. Clark watched her walk gingerly across the icy lot, until he realized who it was.

"Hey!" he called from the street.

Judy looked up. A candy bar slid to the ground. She began walking quickly away from him.

"Wait a minute," said Clark, striding toward her across the slipperiness. "Hold on, there. Hey, listen. I'm not mad. Let's just talk about this for a minute . . ."

But by then Judy was moving at a dead run toward a dark blue beat-up town car by the gas pump, on her face the expression of a gymnast barreling toward her vault. She threw open the car door on the passenger side, and just then a man's head emerged from the driver's side.

Clark stopped. The snow dribbled from the streetlights overhead, falling into his eyes. He smeared his eyes clear. The man stood up, put his fist on the hood of the car, and turned around, saying nothing. His eyes were two shadows, but the expression on his small, protuberant mouth was one of defiance, and complete fearlessness. Clark recognized this expression. He had seen it on the face of James and Judy.

Mr. Nye, sliding his fist off the hood, gave Clark a vague salute. Then, almost casually, he looked up at the sky. "Some night," the man said. Then he gathered his wide, compact shoulders back into the car.

Snowflakes collecting on his shoulders, Clark had watched them go. The car lurched forward and disappeared into the night, spraying clotted snow behind it. He could see two heads in the front seat and a little head in the back, craning around to look, with the same flat but politely concerned expression, getting further away, pulsing under the streetlights as they made for the highway.

The clerk in the blue suit informed him that he would have to pay extra: this was the last room left in town. Everybody was stuck on account of the snow. There was no going in or out of Clementine. The room was supposed to be special in some way. But once Clark settled into the room, which was rather drab except for a canopy bed hung with a limp red swag, and stripped to his underwear, he made an unpleasant discovery. He could see Quail Hollow Road from the window. There it was, those lights on the hill. He pictured her drying dishes languidly at the sink, lank golden hair damp with kitchen steam, and he nearly called out for her. But in that instant his vision shifted and he saw only his face reflected in the glass—his big maw, his suspiciously blue and foolish eyes.

For a Tall Man he went down pretty quickly. He rarely drank, nothing but a little brandy, and the glass bottles seemed small and dainty as potions in a doll's house. One by one, he took them out of the cabinet and drained them. He drank a blue one and a white one and a white one and a brown one and a green one. At first he could tell the difference between them, but soon the flavors blended into one oily swill and he skid off into an opinion-free intoxication. He watched his hands as the sense drained out. After that, wood felt like nothing, hair, like nothing.

At some point, he noticed a painted facsimile of a coat of arms on the wall and began to laugh very loudly. He went to the door where a tin plate read "The Royal Suite." The Royal Suite, he thought. Ridiculous! There wasn't a jot of royal anything in this second-rate city. No kings. No knights. No ladies. Though it was rumored that President Taft, that fattest of presidents, had gotten lost here once on his way somewhere else. This vision of a lost fat president was so hilarious to Clark that, after a while, he heard a voice through the wall groaning, *All right, Jacko. Pipe down already.*

"My God!" said Clark to the wall. "I got the *Royal* Suite. Ha! What's yours called?"

Aww for Christsake, said the voice. *Listen, these walls are paper thin.*

Clark sat down heavily on the bed. "It's just so damned pathetic, you know? How'd I end up in this pathetic town in such a dumb lifetime? I was supposed to be something. My mother thought I was the goddamned crown prince."

The voice in the wall did not respond. Clark rummaged inside the wicker basket, which kept swinging around in his vision, but it was all wrappers and empties. This sobered him a little.

"She's dead, by the way," he told the wall. He slapped his hands over his face. "Jesus Christ!" Then he laughed and fell backward on the bed, thinking of Charlotte's cool white body. "The reason she's so skinny," he said, raising one finger to the ceiling, "the reason is because of her skinny soul." But then he saw her running up and down the stairs laughing, being It, and he had to stand and lean against the wall to steel himself against this sweet image. After a moment the anger came back to him. He liked the strength of it. "She thinks *I'm* a child? And she thinks *I'm* a fool?"

Who cares? said the voice in the wall. *Maybe she's right.*

Clark glowered at the wall. Then after a while he slumped over on the bed.

"At least I'm trying," he said. "I'm trying I'm trying I'm trying."

Hey listen. My girl and me are trying to sleep. Do you want me to come over there and beat the shit out of you?

"Hmm," said Clark to the wall. "Let me think about it."

He pushed himself away from the wall and went to sit at the small chipboard table next to the bed. Aside from the bed and the table, the room contained a fake leather club chair not unlike the one his father used to have in his study. Clark groaned. The last thing in the world he wanted to be reminded of was his father, Wallace Adair. Wallace Adair had an ugly pink cardigan that his mistress Penny Flanigan had knit him. He used to wear it to spite everyone, even himself, it was so damned ugly. At six foot four, he cut quite a figure. A Tall Man with a square jaw in a pink sweater. But Wallace Adair apologized for nothing. He was a man meandering through fire, on fire but not burning. He had the poise and the stealth of a career criminal. His hands were quick, and nothing—once he took it—could be wrested back from him. It's hard not to admire the cruel. After all, they are awesome, and there you are covered in scars.

Once, as a teenager, Clark had seen his father and his mistress together through the window of an ice cream parlor in town.

They were not speaking or touching, but rather passing between them a tall, pink milkshake. She had a pretty, snub nose, a slim waist. She wore a pink jacket the same color as the milkshake. Instead of being horrified, Clark's reaction was strange. He'd found them picturesque, and he had leaned against a lamppost and watched while they shared their treat. Smiling backward at this insensible memory, he was now punching out the numbers on the phone pad, overcome with a wonderful enthusiasm.

The telephone rang numerous times on the other end. Clark listened, mouth open. He chuckled. He could almost see the old man groping around in the dark, cursing.

"Hello? Damn it . . ."

"Dad! Dad!" he laughed. "It's me."

A pause. Then finally, "What in God's name?"

"Well, I'm not calling you in *God's* name, Dad. I didn't mean to wake you up. I didn't notice the time." Clark hiccuped. "OK. I didn't even look at the time, but I bet it's late 'cause it sure is dark."

"*Clark?*"

Clark twisted the phone cord around his fingers. "They don't have clocks in this place. But then, real royalty probably don't have clocks. They probably have a whole person whose job it is to follow them around saying what time it is."

There was a short pause. "Oh Jesus. No. Not you too."

"Not me what?"

"Are you calling from the nuthouse?"

"*No.* No—" Clark laughed, swatting the air in front of him as if the old man was right there. "I'm calling you from the Royal

Suite of the Motor Inn. Hey. If you're not too pissed at me, why don't I come and visit?"

It had only occurred to him just then. Naturally! Why not? He was free now, life blown open, wasn't it? On the other end, shuffling. Muffled explanations. Despite the fact that it was Penny Flanigan's house, Clark had somehow not anticipated the actual presence of Penny Flanigan. They lived together now, by the sea. His dad had moved in with her after Clark's mother died, and now they shared it like a married couple. When you thought about it, they'd been waiting twenty years to be together. Penny Pinkypink with the pink waist and the pink hair, swimming naked in milkshake.

"Man," said Clark. "I'm really sorry. Tell your—Mrs. Flanigan—that I'm really sorry I woke her up."

"Oh, don't be so drunk," snapped Wallace out of nowhere. "Call me in the morning. Call me and we'll talk then. I refuse to chat with you at four in the morning. I'm not your goddamned high school sweetheart."

"Hey hey," Clark said, spinning around in his chair until his butt burned pleasantly. "I was just thinking about you is all."

"Think about me on your own time."

"Thinking about you," murmured Clark, "You and Mom."

Clark was enjoying himself. It was fun to be drunk and call people. It was fun to be a Man on the Run. Nobody's Friend. He smiled with touching arrogance, because it just lasted for a moment before he heard his father's voice respond—flat, low, with that terrible frankness he had forgotten about these years he thought he'd escaped it.

"I'll say this once," Wallace growled. "If you come here, don't you come here with ghosts." The old man's breathing was ragged and almost felt hot in Clark's ear. "Do not try to stir things up. I'm warning you."

Clark swallowed.

"If you come here," said the old man, "come here to dance. We'll take you to the Club. No thanking or apologizing or re-hashing any of it."

"OK," Clark said, holding his head, the two halves of which had suddenly began to march in separate directions. His breath smelled poisonous. He felt his drunkenness slip away like a flirt. "Got it."

There was a pounding in his head. Soon he understood the pounding was actually on the wall, and a voice was shouting *Go to sleep! Go the hell to sleep!* He tried to walk away from the anger, dragging the phone off the table and out of the jack. There, in the window, was his big-nosed stupid earnest face sailing by.

THE ACCIDENTALIST

She stood just inside the small, dark ranch house, her brow pressed against the screen. Dried yellow mums sat in two large casks on either side of the door. Clark walked up and faced her through the screen. He raised his cheap drugstore sunglasses.

"You're so tall!" his father's mistress cried.

"Hello," he said.

"You look like a *tree*. You look like an Indian *brave*. Your father says you have Indian blood in you. Is that true?"

From somewhere inside, the old man's awfully familiar voice rang out, "Everything I say is true."

"Who cares," said the woman, not looking away. "I'll believe anything, long as it isn't dull. Don't you agree? Are you still a very serious boy? I remember you perfectly. Those unusual blue eyes. I'm Penny."

She didn't wear pink at all but rather a black dress printed with orange flowers and capped with short ruffled sleeves. Her hair was grayer than he expected, but she had good, youthful-looking shoulders, the same pretty little nose, and her hips swelled under a tightly cinched belt. She was almost too much, the way she kicked open the screen door so that he had to hop out of the way. She took his hand warmly and then let it go.

"I've always liked you, dear," she said in a lowered voice, touching his arm with the pad of her finger, "but you mustn't pretend to like me if you decide that you don't. I won't take it personally. Most of the time I don't like myself, so you see it would only bring us closer. I'm not afraid of anyone, really. It's something lovely that happens to you when you're old."

"Bring him out to the porch, already," yelled the old man, whose elbow caught in sunlight Clark could see through the dark house. "Bring me the virgin sacrifice!"

"Your father loves you so much, although I know it doesn't always *feel* like love. I have the patience of a stone, you see. That's why I get along with Wallace so well. Do you dance?"

Clark looked at his feet.

"Don't you have any bags, dear?"

"Oh," said Clark. "It was kind of a whim, this trip. I—I was just out for a drive."

"Out for a drive," the woman said, nodding.

After getting his car pulled from the Triplex ditch early that morning, Clark had at long last taken to the road. The sun had come out with a vengeance, shining doubly off the snow, and he had to buy the sunglasses just to see without his head splitting. Several hours south of Clementine, he'd stopped at a bar in a small, undistinguished town. For a while, he'd sat in the bar looking out at the telephone booth outside, which trapped the morning light in its dingy cylinder, with a mounting sense of dread. He had two possible calls to make. Only two people in the whole world were expecting his phone call, and yet he doubted if either of them wanted to hear from him, King of What Next.

When Clark's father recognized his voice over the line, the old man had expressed surprise. "I thought you wouldn't remember in the morning," he said with a sigh.

Clark said that of course he remembered, and was on his way. He was already in Suchandsuch and would be there in an hour.

"And where's your wife, incidentally?" Wallace asked.

"At home," Clark had replied.

"Let me get this straight," said Wallace. "A year goes by and I barely hear a word from you, and now all of a sudden you're out for a drive without your wife, and find yourself coming to see me?"

"Guess so."

"All right," grumbled the old man, "well then that's your story so stick to it. So come prepared to dance, because Penny and I are going to Point Drum tonight and she's very set on having a good time. And if you come, she'll want to dance with you. You can borrow a tie. Have you ever met her?"

"Once," Clark had said. "Dad," and here his voice—*damn it*—had broken on the word. The traffic lapsed and the road was quiet. Clark gazed out of his plastic box, the world through his cheap drugstore sunglasses thick with shadow. "Dad, I—"

"Just please don't thank me for anything," the old man warned. "Don't thank me or ask me to thank you."

"All right."

"Don't simper. Just dance."

And here it was now, emerging from the shadows of the dark house – the old man's high-browed, truculent face. He walked out of the brightness in the back of the porch into the interior hallway, a tall dark silhouette, and moved so quickly forward that Clark's hand hadn't time to close around his, which was dry and hard like a wooden prosthetic, before it was swiftly rescinded and swinging at the old man's side.

"Come on in," the old man said.

Wallace Adair sat on a patio loveseat that was covered with a green rubber sheet and rustled like a diaper. Penny Flanigan sat beside him, crinkling her nose in a rather vacant smile. It was cold but neither of them seemed to notice.

"So," Wallace said. "Tell me about life in your new town, Whatsitsname."

"Clementine."

"Like the miner 49–er? And his daughhhhhter, Clementine. Let's get Penny to sing it. Penny has a lovely voice."

"I sing like a toad," said Penny.

"Light she was and like a fayyrie," prompted Wallace, slapping her thigh with his large hand. "And her shooooes were number nine. Herring boxes without topses . . . da dee dee dee Clementine. Oh my darling oh my darling oh mah darrrrling Clementine. You are lost and gone forever. Dreadful sorry, Clementine."

"That's good," laughed Clark, bobbing his head. "I don't know the song."

"You live there and you don't know the song?" Wallace's

expression was grave. "That's like living in a nudist colony without knowing what an ass looks like."

Penny and Clark laughed but Wallace didn't.

"It isn't much of a town," said Clark, remembering it fondly anyway. "We moved there because of the house. We were just drawn to it. Like the house chose us. Weird." *Weird*, now that he thought of it. "I sent you a photograph? It's small, yellow. Homey, you could say."

"A perfect starter home," said Penny.

"Sure," said Clark, leaning back. "A normal house in a normal place."

"Well, I've never heard of Clementine and I used to live right around there," said Wallace.

"Well it exists all right," said Clark. "It's even got a zoo."

"I adore zoos," said Penny.

"And a statue of Vincent George. He was born there."

"I *adore* mimes!"

"All right," said Wallace, bringing his hand down on the glass end table. "Everybody adores everything. So I'm glad for you. I suppose I should come visit one of these days. But I'm a difficult houseguest. You know how I am. Can't please me. I don't eat anything unless it's got gallons of salt on it. I'm not sure I even like people . . ."

"Wallace is an antisocialite," said Penny, drawing her arm across her body and grasping her cocktail from the glass end table. "He likes to be around people so that he can yell at them. He's surprisingly popular."

"People *love* to be yelled at," said Wallace. "I don't get it." The old man looked over at his mistress and stabbed a finger in her direction. "I like her," he said. "And I like that rebel wife of yours. I liked her from the minute I saw her. A real blue-stocking. I love her screechy ways. I used to love sitting in the kitchen with her at the old house, drinking bourbon. How is she?"

"Charlotte?"

"Yes Charlotte. Charlotte-who-stayed-at-home."

"I've seen pictures," said Penny. "What a beautiful girl. She could cut that hair and sell it for a lot of money."

Clark grasped his drink by the rim, swirled it. He sighed and looked up at the pair, who gazed back. Behind him was the view, at which they kept stealing glances. They owned a square of blue green grass and a row of shadbush and beyond that, a portal-sized view of the bay. Clark could smell the shells and seaweed in the air.

"Well, I've never come to visit you either," Clark said. "And you've been here, what, about a year?"

"I've lived here for five, since I retired," said Penny. "But yes, your father joined me . . . later."

"Right," Clark turned around and took in the view. "Well, this is a really nice place, you two."

"Thank you."

"The view is nice," said Wallace, "but the house is dark and damp and full of Penny's farts and craps."

"Wallace."

"Your *objets trouvés*. The crap you find on the beach," he turned to Clark and explained it. "She finds things on the beach—*crap*—varnishes them, and props them against the walls. This is art?"

"Don't you believe a word," replied the woman, shaking a finger, "Wallace loves his little garrison. Wallace loves it all, even the beach art. You can catch him in the morning, gazing down at the garden over there. When the marigolds start to bloom, he stands there and cheers them on. You can do it! he tells them. That's the Wallace that Wallace doesn't want anyone to know about." Penny smiled and rolled her head against the back of the patio sofa. "Oh Clark, what can we do? We're all secretly enchantable. Our heads are lined with silk, like jewelry boxes."

"I agree with that," said Clark.

Penny stood up and walked to the edge of the porch. The heels of her shoes scraped the smooth concrete. Already she seemed light with drink. Clark liked how the drink made her gentle rather than harsh, as drinking tended to make his father. Though her face was visibly aged, the apples of her cheeks were still high and taut-looking, and her arms seemed extraordinarily hairless, and the little dingbat sleeves on her dress, which were more like ruffled bonnet lids, exposed the balls of her shoulders.

"You know what's pretty, though?" she murmured. "When the fog gets stuck in the yard."

"The fog?" Clark asked.

"It gets stuck in little patches. You can see it in the morning."

"Good Lord," said Wallace. "Let's go to the club."

"But it does. Don't you believe me, Clark?"

"Well, don't ask *Clark*," said Wallace. "Clark'll believe anything."

Then the old man grabbed Penny's arm and bit it while she squealed.

Clark looked away. Suddenly, a sense of shame rushed through his body. What was he doing there? He'd come with such resolution, such will, but what was the resolution, what was the will? I mean, what content? It was the sort of overcharged gesture that bad actors make. He missed his ratty plaid blanket, under whose shade he had recovered his strength last summer, watched the finches through that large window in the living room, watched the hawthorn proffer its white flowers, little white bunches like feather dusters. He missed the finches, missed the hawthorn. And yes, he missed Charlotte. How was even this possible? To miss the person with whom you caught on fire? He could not think of her without thinking of himself. And himself . . . well, he hated that guy.

"Clark?" Penny asked, poking him with her shoe. "Don't you believe me about the fog? Wallace never believes me. He's a skeptic—"

"I'm an occasionalist."

"—and he thinks that everything ought to be disbelieved."

"No dear heart, I'm an occasionalist. I believe that nothing has a *precedent*. I believe that one should treat each moment as if it's never happened before."

"How dreary," Penny groaned. "God forbid we learn anything from the whole of human history." She turned to Clark and plucked at his pant leg. "What are you, Clark? An accidentalist? A breathmintalist?"

"An accidentalist," laughed Clark sincerely. "Yeah. That's what I am."

Penny leaned back on the sofa, so that she was looking down her body at the two men. "I like having you to visit, Clark."

"Thank you," Clark said.

"I've always been very fond of people like you. You're a good sport, and I can tell you sort of believe me about the fog getting stuck in the yard. No one ever believes me. Now *you* tell me something unbelievable."

"Good Lord," said the old man. "Let's go to the club already."

Clark blushed. "I don't know."

Penny clasped her knees. "Come on, you can tell me. I'm an ass!"

"Let's *go*," begged Wallace, his legs opening and closing like wings, rustling the green diaper. "We've got a reservation."

"Pooh the reservation," said Penny, swatting his shoulder. "What does it matter?"

"It's you who wanted to dance."

"I always want to dance. Why does it upset you just now?"

"I'm not upset, I'm hungry."

"Eat a peanut."

"*You* eat a peanut."

"I think there are other people living in my house," said Clark. "Lots of them. All at the same time."

Silenced, the pair looked at him. Wallace fell stiffly back against the cushion. Penny paused, shoe dangling from her toes. Behind Clark was the soft, washer-like sound of the bay.

Finally, Penny began to laugh.

"Unbelievable!" she cried, slapping her thigh, stirring the gauzy hem of her dress. "You almost had me!"

"Yeah," said Clark, smiling. "Almost."

PINK ELEPHANT

The trio sat at a cocktail table near the window. The table was so small that Penny's elbows could touch both men at once, while their knees faced off underneath. Wallace placed his large shoe atop of Clark's, thinking it was the foot of the table, and fifteen minutes later Clark was still waiting for a good time to move it. Once the sun set, the bay looked like a tub of oil, and the moon slid unbroken upon the water. Chinese lanterns were strung over a small dance floor outside. A syrupy, instrumental version of "I'll Be Home for Christmas" played on. No one danced.

"Now, if we introduce you to our friends," Penny cautioned Clark, "don't feel the need to be nice. They're a bunch of geriatrics and they won't remember what you say tomorrow. Besides, you're Wally's son. They'll be surprised that you don't have snakes growing out of your head."

"Damn it," snapped his father. Clark jumped and placed one hand on Penny's arm, in a protective gesture of which he was immediately ashamed.

"Xylophone music again," said the old man, as Clark removed his hand. "It makes my skin crawl. Who in the world considers the xylophone a legitimate instrument? Doesn't any-body remember the piano? Did Tony Bennett live *in vain*?"

"Why don't you put your comment in the comment box, dear?"

"Because it's a gripe, not a comment. Do they have a gripe box?" Wallace turned and nudged Clark with his elbow. "Get ready, Clark. When you're old nobody listens to you. They just string you along until you die." The old man turned to Penny, seized her hand and kissed it.

"Cut it out," said Penny.

"Are you afraid Birch Henderson will get jealous?" Wallace turned to Clark in mock confidentiality. "Penny has Birch Henderson lined up to marry her after I'm dead. A real pooh-bah. A dentist. With a hairpiece."

"At least he dances," Penny sneered back, turning also to Clark, so that the both of them were looking into his ears. She whispered, "Wallace doesn't dance to xylophones. Wallace doesn't dance unless he can be the best dancer on the floor."

"I do not."

"Do too."

"I do *not*."

"Wallace can turn anything into a competition."

"I can not."

"Can too."

"Lies! Women's lies. I'm fabulous."

"You dance *insincerely*."

"I didn't know you danced at all, Dad," said Clark.

The two bodies leaned away from him. Clark took a sip of water in the short, ensuing quiet. He had drawn attention to something sour. He could feel the pair resenting him for it. But he had truly never seen his father dance, not in twenty-nine years of life. He wiped the sweat from his water glass and felt once again ashamed. *He was no fun.* Penny and Wallace moved in a flickering shade and he stood out in the open as he was told—a slow, clear target.

He tried to explain, "I've just never seen you dance, Dad."

"Well," Penny said. She took a sip of wine, looking out into the dining room.

The old man leaned back and narrowed his eyes. His colorless face was cold and flat as a sketch. "I smell an elephant," he said, shaking his finger.

"No you don't," said Penny. "It's your own scandal-mongering."

"But I do. I smell a big pink elephant. What I want to know is, who brought him?"

"*Wallace,*" said Penny.

"Is he under the table?" Bending stiffly, the old man looked under the table. Clark removed his foot from under his father's. The old man lifted his bread plate and sniffed it. He sniffed the air around his son. "Who's got an elephant in his back pocket?"

The waiters at the club wore white coats and tuxedo shirts. Not until their waiter reached the table did Clark see that he was an older black man, with large eyes and freckled cheeks. Clark thought it was repulsive to see a club full of white people being served by blacks, along with a couple of white single-mother types. Clark's mother and Wallace had belonged to a similar club in Carnifex Ferry when Clark was a boy, and Clark had retained a loathing for such places. He remembered pacing outside the ladies' room as a child to catch swinging-door glances of his mother as she smoked, casting long, trance-like glances at herself in the mirror.

"Hello," Clark said warmly. "How are you this evening, sir?"

The waiter looked at Clark without recognition. Then, to Clark's horror, he put his hand on Wallace's sport coat. But Wallace turned stiffly in his chair and smiled.

"David," he bellowed.

"*Da*vid," cried Penny.

"They've got the crap music on again tonight, David."

"I know, Wally. I know," said the waiter, soothing the old man's shoulder with his white-tipped fingers.

Clark blinked. His father's face had been overtaken by a modest and attentive grin, and he clapped his hand around the other man's where it lay. Who was this Wallace Adair—a *nice* man? A happy man? A man who talked to marigolds? A man who liked to be clapped on the shoulder? The same man who had not touched his wife in her coffin but placed, inexplicably, a dollar bill in the pocket of her dress? Had he left all of it behind, who he was, freed by disaster?

"Oh, David," Penny was saying. "Let me introduce you to Wally's son, Clark."

"How do you do?"

Clark nodded. Now that they'd been introduced, David's eyes were full of limpid recognition. Suddenly, he appeared handsome and urbane.

"If Wally won't dance with you, why don't you dance with the young man?" the waiter suggested to Penny. Penny fiddled with her necklace.

"Penny wants to dance with Birch Henderson," said Wallace.

"Good thing for you, Wallace, Mr. Henderson isn't here tonight. He's gone into the city, to visit his daughter."

"I didn't know he had a daughter."

"I didn't know you had a son," said David.

There was another tiny hitch in time after that. Clark noticed that time was starting to stick all over the place. Wallace's enormous hands paused over the breadbasket and his face loosened itself to thought before the hands descended inside the linens and they all went on laughing and talking. Within moments it had been decided that Penny would dance with Clark after dinner, wouldn't he, and wouldn't it be warm enough for her since she was such a filly, and the young man was so tall and just like his father forty years ago and look just now Alfred and Bunny Malcolm had taken to the floor and if *they* could do it . . .

But halfway through the meal Clark reacquired a weariness he'd not felt in months. He did not feel free, having escaped Clementine. In fact, he felt worse. Heavier even than he had that past summer, before he saved the boy. He felt that taking a single step or raising a fork of chicken to his mouth would be a heroic act of which he was incapable. Time favored unhappiness. It slowed you through the awful parts and whisked you through the good ones.

How were you supposed to make it all the way through such a life, never ducking through that tempting little chink in the hedgerow like his mother had? Penny was chatting about a sect of occultists who were rumored to meet in the Drum Point golf course at night. Her teeth were stained pink from wine and she'd begun to hiccup at intervals. The small convulsions made the ruffles on her sleeves hitch upward, as if she were taking flight, and her voice, sweet and happily drifting, curled around Clark like the shoots of a vine curl around a fence post or chair within the course of one hot day, binding him to his seat until he found himself staring openly at his father.

The old man was enjoying himself. Clark hadn't seen the man look so happy in years. He obviously liked to be out and about. Suddenly, it pained Clark, right at the core, that while his poor crazy mother was dead, and he himself was hungover and lost and Charlotteless, his father got so neatly what he wanted. For Wallace, Penny Flanigan had always been the pinkness flashing in the far beyond, past the locked gate. And now here they all were, at Point Drum Country Club, drinking pink zinfandel, as if the fulfillment of one wish sated the need for all wishing, like a prisoner who, once he's scaled the holding wall, looks down at his conspirators with tender indifference.

"Quit staring at me, son."

Clark shook his head. He took a quick breath. His father had said it discreetly, while Penny was calling for more wine, and this seemed a kindness.

Penny turned back to them, still laughing at a joke Clark had not heard, her eyes in merry slits. She sighed.

"Well," she said, to no one in particular, "what a lovely, foggy night."

And it was. The fog had rolled in from the water and was hanging over the dance floor. The Malcolms were still dancing. Mr. Malcolm guided his wife back and forth, stiff-armed and somehow graceful, on the invisible plane.

"I've left Charlotte," Clark said.

He looked at his father. Behind him, through the window, the dancers danced in smoke.

"If I could stay for a couple days, to figure out what to do—"

The old man said nothing. He took a loud sip of his scotch and soda.

"Of course you can," said Penny. "Oh poor dear."

Clark looked down at his plate. Then he turned to Penny and began, helplessly, "I don't know how it happened. One minute we're happily married and the next thing we're arguing all the time and she's drinking in the dark in that *house*, just— staring at me. Like I'm some . . . complete disappointment. And so I try to go out and have a life and help these kids from school and then, okay, so they were stealing from us—oh just crap, who the hell knows? All sorts of strange things have been happening in that house. But maybe it's all in my mind. Maybe it's *me*—"

"Slow down, dear," said Penny.

"And we had this fight and said things . . . So I just got the hell out of there. But because of the snow I had to stay in the Royal Suite and talk to a *wall*," he continued, though he wanted desperately to shut up. He put his hands on his head and stared at the candle flame. "I don't know what the hell I'm doing," he said. "I really don't know what I'm doing. I thought that by my age the right thing to do would just be obvious. I'm not in the damn ballpark."

The old man frowned. Signaling what? Clark was losing the thread of his story.

"*I left my wife*," Clark said more urgently, underscoring the words by rapping on the table with his butter knife. The candlelight flickered on the wall.

Finally Wallace said, "That's it?"

"What?"

Penny put her hand on Clark's. "Oh dear," she said. "You haven't left her."

"*What?*" His voice rose. "I'm here, aren't I? I left."

"The moorings don't give just like that," Penny murmured. "You'll see."

"I see already!"

Penny gathered her hands in front of her calmly, and lowered her eyes as she spoke. Behind her, the waiters moved in the candlelight, quiet as fish.

"A person may create certain things," she began. "A person may create certain bonds that eventually surpass him in strength. The bond takes on a life of its own, like a third life, a child, you build between yourself and someone else. It's mightier than you'll ever be. It's half beautiful, half awful. It's love!" She laughed softly, shrugging. "But it's the only thing immortal about you. Even when you leave, it's still there. Even when you *die*, it's still there. Behind you, as smoke. Love smoke."

The woman's eyes took on a shade. She lifted them, full of years, to her lover, then brushed her lips with her napkin. "Well,

Wally," she said briskly, "There's your pink elephant. Clark and Charlotte, on the rocks."

"No," the man said, shaking his head. "That's not it. That's not the whole elephant."

"Oh come *on*," the woman moaned. "Let's dance. Let's feel good. It's Saturday night! Don't worry, all this crap will still be here when we come back."

The woman tugged on both arms until Clark was standing.

"Will you watch over our crap while we're gone, Wallace?"

"I'll watch the crap. I'll make sure no one takes any."

"But I don't want to dance!" cried Clark.

"You sound just like your father," Penny said, pulling him toward the floor, where dancing couples moved half-obscured, in and out of the fog.

THE DAMAGE

Clark was looking at Penny's scrapbook of dried flowers the following afternoon when his father stood up and hitched his pants. "My boy," he said. "You're my favorite fool." Clark paused with his finger pointing appreciatively at a flattened gardenia. It was the afternoon, the sun was edging across the yard, and all of a sudden Clark realized his father was telling him something true. He had not come all the way there to look at dried flowers. He had not come to make nice with his father's mistress, going rock hounding, rolling over like a dog to her affection. In fact, the invigorating violence that had spirited him out of Clementine and onto the road to his father's house before he even knew where he was headed had absconded and left him with a faint kiss mark, and he felt again that he was standing on nothing. Here he was, a fool, looking at dried flowers with the two people whose love had killed his mother, as if he were being shown the very evidence against them.

And yet Clark did not leave. He physically could not. He thought of Charlotte and felt her, but then just as readily he stuffed her back down into some kind of invisible hole. Four days into his stay, even Wallace seemed to accept this, pacing with his scotch around the willow trunk, at intervals taking in a breath of air so cool and briny it must have penetrated the dead space—the skeptical, occasionalist deadness inside him. Christmas was fast upon them and it seemed that the old man was becoming resigned to sharing the holiday with his son.

Later, Clark lay on his twin bed with one arm propped behind his neck, his feet hanging off. His room was the last on the hall, a dark small room with a bookshelf of moldering mystery novels, which he had begun to read. He took care to keep the room and bed neat, and to pair his shoes, and to come quickly when called. Yet he also felt safe doing nothing, like some overgrown child, alone and absorbed.

"Hello." Penny poked her head through the open door. Her hair was loose, betraying its soft thinness.

Clark put down his book. "Hey. What can I do?"

"I need your help with something," Penny said. "Follow me."

He followed her down the hall toward the living room, his long shadow trailing behind, until they reached the small blue spruce, decorated with seashells that Penny and Clark had found on the beach. Underneath the Christmas tree sat a modest collection of gifts.

Clark laughed. "If Charlotte was here, she'd be shaking those boxes all day long." He walked around the tree admiringly. "She can't stand guessing. Wrapped things make her crazy."

"Hold this," said Penny, handing him an ornament. "I bet she wouldn't mind knowing where *you* are."

Clark pursed his lips, looking at the tree.

"Have you phoned her yet?"

"No," said Clark.

Penny turned to the crate and began to rummage in it noisily. She withdrew an angel made out of driftwood with a painted face and gold foil wings. She gave him the angel.

"I need you to put him up there."

"When I was a kid, I used to make ornaments too."

"Really?"

"Hobby horses made out of socks, painted tin cans. I found a whole box of homemade Christmas ornaments when Mom died. She had kept them, every one. Then again, she also kept boxes of old pantyhose and used aluminum foil. She had a little problem, you know, throwing things out. She thought someone was examining our trash."

Penny placed a chair before the tree. Clark stepped heavily onto the seat.

"Anyway," he said. "It's all in the dump. Mary and I took it all to the dump."

Clark secured the angel on top of the tree. Turning his head, he looked out the window. He saw his father coming up from the water in a wooly cardigan. Addled steps. Greasy head bent. Those large stiff paws, swinging at his sides. Clark looked away.

"You know, I saw you once," he said, standing on the chair. "When I was a kid. Through the window of an ice cream parlor. I thought you were pretty."

He stepped down from the chair, when to his enormous surprise, Penny grasped him by the shoulders. Her lips were clenched white around the edges, and the cords of her neck stood out. She held him so hard he almost had to laugh. His hands were retracted awkwardly at his chest.

"You make me so sad," she said, her voice shaking. "The way you are. You lay yourself bare. Don't you know people hate that? Poor child. Why are you so careless with yourself?"

Terrified, Clark looked out the back door. He wanted to push her away.

"I really must tell you something," she said. "You were a patsy. You and Mary and my kids too. We set you up. The world was our responsibility, you see. But we had you and then we passed off the world to you. All our miseries. Finally, we didn't care about you enough. Even your poor mother didn't care about you enough. We were all . . . elsewhere." She let her arms down and her whole person seemed to slump, as if her very juice—her pinkness—ran off through her fingertips.

"And so I apologize. For all of us. You know of course your father never will, and your mother . . . can't. I'm sorry," she said. "Maybe it's too late for me to say that now. But not for you. It's not too late for you. You could be trusted, if you were to say, for whatever you've done or not done so far, that you were sorry. That you were truly, truly sorry. You could *mean* it. Have it matter. *Surely* you could be braver than us . . ." Penny bent her head. "When your mother passed, life went on so unyieldingly. We watched it. We knew we'd follow soon, and just like her, leave mostly damage. We would end, but the damage . . . The damage—"

She sobbed once, then backed away, laughing.

"It's not like that," said Clark. "It doesn't have to be."

"Well then *do* something, Clark," she cried. "Quit cooperating!"

Wallace rattled at the back door. His head was invisible behind the pink valance.

"I don't quite understand," said Clark.

Penny looked toward the door, tears making tracks down both cheeks. Then she flung her hand out, and walked from the room.

"Oh, let him come," she said.

Clark gazed at the Christmas tree. The angel sat cockeyed atop it. Penny was disappearing down the hall. She walked with both hands underneath her hair, on her neck. Wallace rattled the back door again. "Goddamn it, open the door." The old man stood gripping the lapels of his sweater. He was bent over, trying to see under the valance.

"You," he said, pointing. "Come out here. And bring us a drink."

The day outside was unseasonably warm for December. A group of children walked down the street with a creel and a landing net, moving out toward the beach at Point Drum. Clark, after nestling a scotch and soda in his father's great claw, waved at them and they waved back.

Wallace patted the patio chair at his side.

"Come sit by your old man," said Wallace.

"My pleasure," said Clark.

They sat and watched the portal-sized view of the bay. Across it sluiced a tiny ketch. Underneath the wind and rustling poplar leaves, the erratic *chang chang* of a buoy.

"It's good of you to let me camp out here," Clark said. "I know I'm a grown man but it's nice to be a son, too. Just hangin' around, washin' the car. Life was pretty damned simple once."

The old man nodded.

"I want you to know, Dad," said Clark. "I have a plan. I'm going to . . . I'm going to get my life together. I'm close to making the right decisions. I've been protecting myself, and great men don't protect themselves. They don't have contingencies. Know what I mean?"

Clark heard a nervousness in his own voice. He fought to keep from looking at his father. The Plan, he thought. Just tell him about the Plan.

"I've finally decided, since I've been here, that I'm going to quit my job after Christmas vacation is over. That is, if they haven't fired me already." He wished he had a glass or something to hold. "Who wants to sit around writing testimonials for soccer camp? Not me!" He laughed, incapable of staying aground, the Plan already shredding up behind him, but he hoped his father would approve of it anyway and say, You can do whatever you put your mind to son. "Not to say my life is extraordinary, but I was doing all right there for a while this summer. I was feeling charmed. Special. I was feeling heroic. This sleepy person I'd become lately—he disappeared and I became like a new man. But then, I don't know what happened. I keep losing the feel of him, whenever I get close . . ."

Clark stopped, realizing he'd wandered into a realm of metaphors or poetry where his father would refuse to follow. He wanted to describe bounty. But suddenly he wasn't convinced of that, of what he meant by that. He stole a look at the old man, who wore a tolerant grin, like a cleric.

"I've always wanted to work for a newspaper."

"Well, that'd be fine," his father said.

"Really? You think so?"

"Sure. It's all fine and it's all awful. If I'd have had a choice, I would have retired forty years ago."

Clark nodded. The front door creaked open then shut. They heard the sound of Penny's wooden clogs on the front walkway.

"So," said his father. "Would you like to have it out now?"

"What's that?"

"Would you like to have it out now or keep stalling?"

"I don't . . ." stuttered Clark. "I don't know what you mean."

"Come *come*. Why don't you just let me have it like you planned? You've dawdled long enough now." Wallace looked at his watch, then touched his son's arm with his hard fingers. "You've been here for days. Tell me you didn't drive down here just to hang out and wash the car. You want something from me."

The old man leaned back and spoke to the ceiling. "Listen," he said, "you don't love your wife, she doesn't please you, or you—you don't please her? You don't enjoy the look of her anymore, or she kind of jumps at your touch? Don't blame me for it." Suddenly, his voice hardened and dropped from the air like hail. "You listen to me, don't you blame me for your ridiculous ambitions. I never lied to you. It was her. *Her.*"

And then, his eyes squeezed shut, he could see her. Vera. Not when she was young and happy, but when she was old and uncombed and in her white nightgown. She rose up, as easy as that, her gray-blue eyes aglow with wonder at her own reduced circumstances.

"Your mother thought life was supposed to be perfect," the old man remembered with narrowed eyes. "You should have seen her face whenever any little thing went wrong. She was a paranoiac, you know. They can treat it easily now. But she refused to see a doctor! That one time in Florida, I had to trick her. You poor kid, you thought we were on vacation. Your mother ran away from the facility three times and I had to go find her while you kids played on the beach. It all started after your poor sister Mary was born. She started to accuse me of stealing things. Whenever Mary crawled around the corner, she'd say, 'The baby! You stole the baby!' I was surprised we even made a baby, given how infrequently she allowed me into her bedroom. We weren't *happy* after that. Then you came along. For a while, I wasn't sure you were an actual human child. With all her crazy stories, I worried that maybe we had made you up. As if you were born out of madness."

Clark coughed and sat up in his chair. He felt an incredible desire to get back in the car and speed away, to keep driving, to never stop. He looked at the old man, terrified.

"Listen, Dad," he said. "We don't have to go into all this. It strikes me as . . . It strikes me as unfair, to talk about her now, when she can't defend herself."

"Don't insist that things be fair, damn it. You're a man now. Only a *child* insists that things be fair." And like a second blow, it was the word "child" that debilitated him, and he understood violently that he was foundering, like a ship, that he had been foundering this whole time, this whole year since the death, with too much pride to say so even in the privacy of his own mind. He simply wished to be dead if that would end this conversation. He bit his cheek and looked away. Tears would only make the old man angrier.

"But never mind recent history," continued Wallace, shaking some image from his head. "Too soon to understand it so don't try. Let me tell you about your mother. You should have seen her when she was young and healthy. She was the shiniest, glowingest thing, without a nick. She had hair down to her bottom and she washed it—I guess you know how she washed it—with valerian root. She had this fantastic royal air. She could be queen of the dullest situations. Queen of the barbecue. Queen of the rumpus room. When she fell into one of her moods, back when they were just moods, I would say, A penny for your thoughts, love, and she would turn and say, Dearest, my thoughts are worth *at least* a dollar." Wallace laughed softly. "At least a dollar! She was so young. She wanted to move out of her awful daddy's house. I was just the ticket. I was significantly older than she—"

"Just like Penny," Clark protested, half to himself. "Penny's young too."

His father turned and looked at him levelly.

"I'm just saying," Clark muttered.

"What is this to you," said his father in a low voice. "Paint by numbers? My loving son, you have to hear the whole story. The one you came here for. Isn't this what you came here for?

Your mother has been dead one year almost to the day. Don't look at me as if you'd forgotten."

Clark looked away. He had forgotten. And he had not forgotten at all.

"Anyway," said Wallace. "Your mother was the shiniest thing, and I was a foolish dandy. But it was the end of dandyism by then. All of a sudden you weren't allowed to cut your hair anymore or walk a woman by the arm. The haberdashery closed in Carnifex Ferry. I refused to live in a town where you couldn't buy a suit that actually fit you. Also, there had been another woman there. Someone else before Penny."

"Good God, Dad," said Clark, standing up. "All right. Let's stop. I didn't mean to upset you by coming here. I don't know why I came. I didn't have anywhere to go when I left Charlotte."

"No, that's *not* why you came. I'm *telling* you why you came. It's not about Charlotte. Sit down. Sit down. Now quit avoiding this, for Christ's sake. You started it."

"You started it!"

"I did not. I did *not*. I did not show up mysteriously at your door, thinking I might catch you unawares, in the Christmas spirit, so that I might play upon your old man's guilt. You think I'll get softer as I go? When I face my death? You think I will love you well then? I don't have *time* to be different, Clark. Look at me. Look at me. Look out there. What is that?"

"That? A tree. A tree."

"And that?"

"Jesus, Dad."

"What is it?"

"A car."

"That's right. A car. And over there, that's a house. It's just a word but it's all we've got. House. Car. Tree. Out there, water. Boats. Fish. Up, up. Look up! That's called the sky. Down here, at our feet, the ground. I tried to tell you all this. I tried to tell you but you were stuck in a dream. You were stuck in *her* dream. This is what I want to say to you, Clark. Now that you've come here I realized I want to tell you something. It's this. No! Don't wiggle in your chair. It's this: I am glad for you that she's dead."

"Please!" Clark clutched his head. The grief made his sight darken. "I don't want to *talk* about it."

"Listen!" Now the old man was leaning toward him, so that Clark could feel his breath. "What do you think will kill me but the guilt of it? My hair falls out in handfuls and my fingers are swollen and rotting off at the knuckles. Part of me has decayed. But I don't care! I don't care about me. Because I don't care about anyone. You were the one aberration. You were the gaff. I made you with her and you were my son and I couldn't help it. It wasn't the same with Mary. When you were an infant I used to weep when *you* wept—why had I subjected you to this world, knowing what I knew? Such a good little baby, so full of love—a mere *sac*rifice. There, you have my confession. Any parent would say it if he weren't so damned doe-eyed. But Clark," the man leaned forward and slowed his words, "I have to tell you that you have become a fool. You are a waste of my guilt. I wanted to be a God but I got dime-store feelings like everyone else. And you aren't even worth those. Because you had a chance and you lost it. Do you know what chance I mean?"

"No," Clark whispered.

"You don't know, even now? Even now when you could lose your marriage and your job and your life?"

"No. No, I don't. I'm sorry."

"Do not apologize to me, goddamn it! You *know* I hate that. I will *never* apologize to you. Look at me. I'm Wallace Adair. I'm just an old man who will leave this world as wicked as he found it."

Then, with his hard, balled-up fist, the old man struck Clark on the arm. A shock of stiff gray hair fell down on his forehead.

"Jesus Christ, Dad. Don't *hit* me."

"How could I help you?" cried the man, bringing down his hard fist again. "You had the shape of water! And then—a miracle, disguised as a tragedy—she died! That was your chance. She set you free! It was the most generous thing she ever did! What astonishes me, what drives me crazy, is you might not even take a run for it when *I* die. You'll just go blundering around the world, looking for a new jail."

"I'm warning you, Dad. Don't hit me again. I'm stronger than you!" And just like that the man swung out with his other hand, and Clark caught the fist and squeezed it until the knuckles cracked. But the sound made Clark flinch, for he had not intended to squeeze so hard, and the old man took the opportunity to club him with his loose half-opened fist, right on the ear, which set off a dim ringing in his head, and Clark was paralyzed less by the blows than by the long-stoppered enthusiasm from which they issued. A more ambitious blow caught him on the neck, in the tenderness below his Adam's apple, and he hollered in disbelief, "Stop!"

But Wallace Adair did not stop. Clark leaned back into the chair, eyes wild. His horror was so great that he did not even think to raise an arm in defense. He only watched this furious motion, his father's stiff hair now in his eyes, so that he struck out almost blindly, twice punching the wooden chair back beside Clark's face.

A high note arose, a long held grieving note. Clark did not know where it was coming from until he saw Penny's two small shoes in the doorway. A woman's wailing. Penny lurched onto the patio, stomping and shrieking, her hair falling over her shoulders. In her hand, she wielded a pair of garden shears. Over Wallace's head, the blades glinted.

"I'll stab you!" she screamed.

Wallace looked up at her the first time without seeing her. He turned back to his son and kept swinging blind, and now Clark could see his father's eyes brimming beneath his hair. The blades flashed like a searchlight across the patio floor, and yet the old man wrestled and swung without seeing. Penny grunted as she fought herself. "Wally!" she screamed. When the old man looked up again, he looked past the garden shears, and his expression changed to that of affectionate recognition, as if his lover was coming to deliver a kiss. The light from the blade crossed Wallace's eye.

And then he stopped. The old man paused with his swollen hands retracted as if from heat. Then he slumped back into his chair and turned his sunspotted head away, toward the water.

For a moment, no one moved.

Wallace began to fumble at his collar, his breathing ragged. Penny looked up at her hand. The shears clattered on the concrete porch. She knelt by Wallace and worked her trembling fingers around the top button of his shirt. Clark watched this,

this woman biting her sweaty lip as her fingers wrestled with the tiny button. His father's legs opened and closed like butterfly wings. His hands searched the air. The buttons rolled across the concrete, and at last the old man caught his breath, and Penny collapsed on the concrete porch, her slip showing.

Again, no one spoke. Clark lifted his hands from his knees, where they had remained unmoving. He touched his lip. A drop of blood fell from his lip onto the collar of his shirt.

"Dad?" he whispered.

Penny stood. "I'll get him some water," she said.

Clark looked at the side of his father's face. "Dad?" he whispered again.

Wallace shook his head. In one, immodest gulp, he fit the air down his throat, and his voice came surging out, "It's just a rattle, I said, it's just this loose thing I have a loose thing in my throat."

Penny reemerged with a glass of water. As she placed it in Wallace's hand, he caught her hand with the other. She leaned backward, grunting. But the old man held her fingers fast. Fondly, persistently, he stroked them, one by one, then let her go.

The bay crashed. Father and son sat alone, still inclined toward one another from the blows. Clark could not remove his eyes from the side of his father's head.

Finally the old man spoke. "Oh don't . . . look at me like . . . that like I'm a hypocrite, just because I love her . . . little fingers."

The old man's breath smelled bad. The smell made Clark feel physically ill. At last, he stood, upsetting his chair, and put his brow against the porch screen. Then he thrust the porch door open with one hand and bent over.

"Let it out," the old man said.

"Shut up," whispered Clark, closing his eyes.

Behind him his father said, "What else is there? Hmm? What else have you found, Clark, my pilgrim, my . . . counselor? Tell me at heart you don't live for the sound of your wife . . . clearing her throat in the next room. Tell me that's not true. Because you know there is nothing else but that . . . to tell the children in school when they ask you . . . but what holds life *together*? And you can only think, 'love.' Love no matter . . . what. Having someone with whom . . . you double your chances. Someone to accompany you through this difficult . . . world."

"Don't," said Clark, not turning around. "Don't talk, Dad. Let's just sit here. Let's sit here, then I'll go."

"Hey now. Don't . . . go," he panted. "She's making dinner."

"I don't want to stay."

"Stay for dinner."

"No."

"Stay, and then go. Then, that'll be it. We'll be through with all of it . . ."

"*Do not talk to me!*" shouted Clark, lurching toward his father with a clenched fist.

The old man winced. But then, just as quickly, he smiled.

"There you go," Wallace said. "That's the spirit." He crossed one yellowed ankle over his knee, showing the worn out sole of his loafer. Grasping the top of his glass, he swirled his watery drink. Then he looked out toward the bay.

"I wish I believed in God, son. Then at least I could look forward to meeting . . . someone interesting." Wallace coughed and rubbed himself against the seat. "But I don't think so. I think our souls evaporate, and are undone, like millions of knots. I think there is nothing after life.

"But dear son, if I'm entirely wrong, if there is a God and he runs a heaven, I'm sure your beloved mother, who I know you loved with all your heart, I'm sure . . . she's there, sawing away at her viola. You were so . . . generous. You always saw through to the woman she could have been, were not the tables turned against her." The old man took a sip of his drink, and finally, his breathing became even.

"The viola," Wallace laughed, remembering. "She was terrible at that instrument, wasn't she? But you clapped. You clapped and clapped. And maybe in heaven she . . . maybe . . ." He looked up at his son, with an expression of complete sincerity, "Maybe in heaven your love makes her brilliant."

The old man raised his glass to the sky.

"To you, my darling," he said. "To you."

GRIEF

Grief is long, flat roads and low skies. Grief is ashes. Distant carnival music. Roadside cats weak with hunger. True grief, he sees, is shocking.

But maybe, he thinks, After . . .

He drives the long, flat road under the low sky that is like a shelf of ash. Along the roadside trots a gaunt yellow cat. As he drives, he begins to cry. The carwheels thumping in their wells go Re*mem*ber? Re*mem*ber? Re*mem*ber? His remembering gathers like a storm in his mind. The sky darkens. The clouds gather. Yes, Florida—of course it was not a vacation. Gray beaches and gray music, and games that were not games. He sees now how easily he has believed in the happiness of tiny windows, tiny distractions, chinks of blue sky. Worse, he sees that resistance to grief is grief twice. He will have to weep twice. Once for now, and once for Florida. He will have to drive the long flat road twice.

Pulling into the Drive-Thru, he leans out the window toward the speaker.

"I'll take a coffee," he says, wiping his nose with his sleeve.

That it? responds the adolescent voice.

"Yes," Clark says. "Black."

That'll be ninety cents. Pull up to the second window, please.

As he pulls forward, he sees, just off to the side, a public telephone. He swerves toward it, gets out, slips his quarters into the slot. As the phone begins to ring, he pulls his collar up against the coming rain.

Back at home, she stirs. Her sleep is very thick and glutinous. It is not sleep. She totters on the edge of sleep and something very, very different. Beside her, the bottle of pills lies upended. How many were there? Five? Twenty? Her vision pulses. The house slips out from under her. She looks down at its roofless shell and sees the staircase and the bed, white as a marble bier. It is as if she has jumped very high and been caught in the air. It is silent where she is. And cold. She looks around—*space*. Sheer space, inflationary space. She cries out, but her voice is feeble. All around her the stars prick at her. How she misses the ground! That unassuming yellow house where she keeps herself! To be alive and to walk on dirt. To receive the gifts of pennies and bread and stamps and oranges and kisses. She does not want it to be over. She wants to be alive, a woman who can run and argue and prick herself on things. A woman who can be left even. For wasn't it worth it? Wasn't it something? Hoovering in space, she thinks of this, smiling a little.

Suddenly, in the darkness below, the sound of a telephone.

Wait! she cries. *Hold on! I'm coming back!*

She kicks and kicks but doesn't propel herself any closer to the house. The phone continues to ring but she cannot reach it. It is amazing to her, how far away it sounds, in this death-drugged stupor. Then, suddenly, some force begins to close the blinds to her view, closing the lid or curtain that obscures the entrance.

A mistake! she cries. *I want to come back!*

The house swings in the dark. The phone stops ringing. Exhausted, she stops kicking and gazes down at the silence, floating backward, her arms outstretched.

He hangs up, gets back into the car, and drives up to the second window. It's a gusty, gray day, not yet raining but spitting, and colorless leaves sticking to the windshield wipers as they move back and forth, *thwop thwip thwop.*

The teenage kid at the window winces when he sees Clark.

"Ninety cents," the kid says, touching his visor.

The teenager accepts the money, then hesitates.

He says, "You all right, sir? You need help or something? You look sort of bad."

"Yep," says Clark, taking his coffee. Tears cling to his cheeks and his cuffs are full of snot. "It's pretty bad, all right." But with this admission, Clark laughs. "But I gotta go. I gotta do something."

"Well," says the kid, smiling. "Good luck. Merry Christmas."

He pulls out of the Drive-Thru and turns back onto the long flat road and keeps driving. The hum of the wheels on the road is mesmerizing. The road is so flat and straight it appears to have been crushed by the fact of the sky.

The kid leans out of the window, looking after him.

RAIN

Trees stirred. Birds fell silent. A wasp fretted in a corner. In the sky, thin clouds furled opened like young girls' hands. In the distance, a wind was blowing. The branches clattered, and all at once the wind came up over the hill and washed across the maples in the front yard, and the chimney pot atop the yellow house on Quail Hollow Road started slapping.

She heard the trees. She heard the chimney pot. The house creaked in the wind. In this way she knew she had survived. Because what god would be clever enough to bury her along with the sounds of her life?

Cautiously, Charlotte opened one eye. It parted at the crusted seam, and there was a slight tugging pain. Overhead, the ceiling was blank. The crack did not move, and the room itself did not move or shudder. She caught her breath and closed her eyes, stroking the exquisite flatness of the sheets. There was never an object as beautiful as a bed. A strange cry escaped her mouth. She felt her tongue with her fingers. Her tongue slapped numbly in her mouth, which tasted of chemicals. She could not feel her tongue. She poked it. Her tongue was not working but her fingers were, and her heart was beating and she was alive. And now she smelled, as if in a dream, the smell of toast. Weakly, she pulled the blanket aside and sat up.

"Hi," Clark said.

Charlotte screamed and covered herself with the sheet.

For there he was—born of thin air, sitting tall in the dim gray sunlight, his olive skin damp and hair mussed with wind and travel. His shirt was rumpled and stained, and she could see his neck and his breastbone moving with his breath. On his lap, he held a plate of jelly toast. She reached out to him, then withdrew her hand. Fingers to her lips, she stared.

"I was just sitting here," Clark said, "watching you sleep. And for some reason I remembered this joke. I thought it would make you laugh. Can I tell it to you?"

Charlotte looked down. She looked up, eyes wide. Imperceptibly, she nodded.

He sighed and pressed his lips together, wiping his mouth with his sleeve.

"Okay," he said. "There are these two guys stranded on a deserted island. They've been stuck there for years, you know, eating barnacles and coconuts and hoping to be rescued. But no one ever comes. One day, they find a genie in a bottle. The genie says I will grant you both one wish. He says to the first guy, What do you wish?"

He smiled a little, looking off toward the doorway. "Christ, cries the guy. I wish to be rescued, of course. And as soon as he says it—poof, the guy disappears. The genie says to the second guy, I will grant you one wish. What do you wish? The second guy looks around. He looks around at the island, the coconut trees. It's terrible to be on the island all alone. He misses his friend. Gosh, the guy says to the genie, I sure wish my friend were here."

He looked at Charlotte and laughed shyly. Then he continued, more softly. "I always really liked watching you sleep. Do you know you kind of purse your lips? I think it's going to rain. I just beat it here, I think." He gazed over his shoulder out the window, scratching his neck, suddenly awkward.

Charlotte blinked back at him. After a moment, she moved over on the mattress. She pat the space beside her.

"Oh yeah?" Clark said.

Charlotte nodded. The bed creaked as he sat. He passed her the plate of jelly toast and smiled.

"Hungry?" he said. "Well, eat up. Merry Christmas, Charlie."

She tried to take the plate, but her hands trembled so wildly that she couldn't hold on to it. Clark caught the plate in the air and looked at her.

"Are you all right?" He touched her forehead. Then he drew his hand away in alarm. "Jesus, you're *soaked*. Jesus, Charlotte. Jesus! Are you sick? Let me open a window."

He lumbered to the window and opened it. The air rushed in.

"I missed you," she said suddenly from the bed. "I missed you so much."

"What?" Clark said. "I can't understand you."

"I missed you. I love you. I've loved you since I was a child. I dreamed of you when I was a child," she laughed, wiping the corner of her eye with her wrist. "I missed you, Clark. You and all of it. Toast. Oranges."

"What?" Clark leaned forward on the bed, slapping one hand to his head. "Your words are all slurry, Charlotte. I can't understand a thing you're *saying*." His mouth was trembling. "What *happened* to you?"

She shook her head no.

"I *love* you," she said, laughing clumsily. "That's what happened."

"You what?" he said. "Lorloo?"

"I love you!" She was laughing.

He gripped her hand. "Hey, tell me later, all right? Rest for now."

Clark stood up and rubbed his hands together, his brow in a knot. He drew the sheets up to Charlotte's chin. Then he drew them down. He looked desperately around the room as if expecting someone else to spring helpfully out of the wall. He stumbled into the bathroom and clawed through the medicine cabinet. He came out into the room empty handed, breathing hard.

"A sweater," he said, pulling one down from her closet. "You should have some clothes on so you don't catch a chill."

She raised her arms up and he pulled the sweater over her head. Her face popped through the other side, looking up at him, eyes soft and watchful and urgent about something. He pulled her hair out and smoothed it against her back. With the cuff of her sweater, she touched the rawness on his lip.

"Oh that," he said, looking down. "You should see the other guy."

He sat next to her on the bed, their arms touching.

The wind fell still. The chimes hushed. Everything was listening.

Clark cleared his throat. "I'm sorry," he said.

Charlotte swung her head in his direction, mouth opened. Then she played with the cuff of her sweater.

"It's good you can't talk," he said.

She laughed.

"I'm sorry," he said. "I'm sorry, Charlotte. For everything. I'm sorry that I went away. And I'm sorry for everybody, for the things that happen. All the . . . blows. And we hardly even know. . . . We don't even *feel* them when they . . ." He paused, one hand in the air, and gasped. Suddenly, leaning forward, a great pressure broke in his gut. A breaking rolling opening. He pressed Charlotte's hand to his eyes and sat hunched over that way for a moment, breathing into the palm of her hand.

The word itself, he saw then, was like a password. With it, he entered innumerable rooms. He said it again. He wanted to.

"Oh, Charlie," he said, weeping now. "I'm so sorry."

She pulled him into her arms. There they sat, rocking each other.

Finally, it began to rain. It began as a tapping on the windowpanes of the neighborhood. Then, all at once, the sky broke, rushing down in great warm spouts, pouring from the gutters, jumping up and down on the drowning streets. Leaves and coupons and newspapers in their plastic sleeves swam in swollen puddles, and Christmas lights blinked dimly through the sheets of rain.

And outside, in the yard, in the downpour, were Clark and Charlotte Adair. They were shrieking. They were soaked. Clark slammed the car trunk shut and stepped toward his wife, who looked back up at him with licks of hair pasted to her cheeks. She was laughing. She was spinning around and around in the yard, in her nightgown and loose, oversized sweater. Rain flew from the ends of her yellow hair.

Clark clapped, looking on.

She was spinning. She looked like a girl on the first day of spring. The rain, warm and constant, felt like some first rain. She spun closer to him until she fell against him, wet and laughing and dizzy. They staggered now to the car, and Clark helped Charlotte inside. He tossed a duffel bag in the backseat, where Tecumseh was awaiting them quietly, sniffing the air through the gap in the window, showing a respectful yet dispassionate interest in it all—laughter, life and death, the scent of moss.

Clark stood and squinted back at the house. The house looked on with a dark, misty expression. Rain ran into his eyes, and at first he was not sure of it. Charlotte was mopping her face with a napkin from the glove compartment.

"Look," he whispered.

And there they were—it was them all right—in the upper windows, the one chasing the other. The pale hair fluttered past like ribbons. The second figure persued, draped in a blanket, arms outstretched like a monster—a benevolent monster at large, lumbering after all the delicious human embraces.